a rose by any other name

a rose by any other name

M.H. SALTER

DAYTIME MOON PUBLISHING

Copyright © 2016 M.H. Salter

Excerpts from *Romeo and Juliet* by William Shakespeare

Sonnet 76 by William Shakespeare

Book cover design by Damonza

Edited by Paul Hines

eBook ISBN: 978-0-9925267-5-7

Print Edition ISBN: 978-0-9925267-4-0

First published 2016 by Daytime Moon Publishing

Contact the author at: www.mhsalter.com or mhsalter@daytimemoon.com.au *also by m.h. salter*

Doorways
Dove – The Freedom Series: Book One

about the author

Melanie Hyland Salter lives in Adelaide with her husband, three children, two dogs, and an army of cats.

Her novel, *Dove*, was shortlised for the Impress Prize for New Writers, and received an Honourable Mention in the PeaceWriting Awards.

Her short story, *Mountain Man* (retitled *Frozen Souls*), was published in Dark Edifice #2, and was Highly Commended by the Australian Community Writers Inc. Her short story, *Sunrise Lake*, won first prize in the Away With Words Short Story Competition and was published in the accompanying anthology. Her short story, *The Saving Grace*, was Highly Commended by the NYC Midnight Short Story Challenge. These can be found in the short story anthology, *Doorways*.

Melanie has a BA in Writing, and a Diploma of Professional Writing. She is registered on the Australian Society of Authors as a Mentor for fiction writers.

Contact her at mhsalter@daytimemoon.com.au

This book is dedicated to Glenda and Chris
for never was there a story of more woe.

sonnet 76

Why is my verse so barren of new pride,
So far from variation or quick change?
Why with the time do I not glance aside
To new-found methods, and to compounds strange?
Why write I still all one, ever the same,
And keep invention in a noted weed,
That every word doth almost tell my name,
Showing their birth, and where they did proceed?
O! know sweet love I always write of you,
And you and love are still my argument;
So all my best is dressing old words new,
Spending again what is already spent:
For as the sun is daily new and old,
So is my love still telling what is told.

~William Shakespeare

prologue

Destiny swirls and plinks inside my crystal ball like a moth against a window, eager to break free and influence the future of the soul to whom it is attached.

Across the velvet wall of my tent, candle light flickers and enters every bead in the curtained doorway. The tiny glass orbs shine, as if each one holds within it a separate prophecy. I gaze through this glowing doorway – a doorway that divides the present from the future – and I wait for Delia Rose's uncertain form to appear.

As I know they will, our two worlds finally meet, coming together like lovers' lips in a first hesitant but unstoppable kiss. And when she steps forward, finally tangible into my reality, I smile to her. As best I can, anyway. For it is hard to smile into the beatific face of impending tragedy. And oh, yes, she is beatific. With her skin as pale as her bleached hair, and her owl-wide eyes as black as the mysteries she is about to learn, she has an aura of serenity that calms even me, even when I know what I am about to do to her.

'Have a seat, child,' I say, even though I wish she would not sit but would instead turn and run as far away from me and my truths as possible, for no one wants to pronounce upon someone else a death sentence.

'Welcome,' I say. 'My name is Mab.'

Delia lowers herself across from me. Her gaze flicks, wild as the candle flames, lighting briefly upon everything but my eyes.

'I'm Delia,' she whispers.

I nod, as if I don't already know her name. 'Twenty dollars, please, Delia.'

With shaking fingers, she slides the note across the table. Then, imitating me, she leans forward, trying to discern what truths lay ensconced in the cold glass orb between us.

'There is a prophecy here,' I whisper. 'You carry it with you.'

'I carry a prophecy?'

'Yes, child,' I say.

I try to hold my words trapped, to spare her the knowledge of her own demise, but I am, as always, unable to control it. My mouth opens and the words march forth with the solid beat and unyielding force of an army. 'An age-old spite will once again be rife among those who've branched from the first quarrel. The streets will flow with crimson's tide of life, and stain the hands and minds of those moral. From each side of this battlefield romance will bloom between you and one forbidden. Your love will break the spell of hatred's trance, and uncover a secret long hidden. Bitterness dissolved, and old wounds healed, this peace will come at a grave and mortal price: two deaths. This noble bargain will be sealed; hatred buried by love's self-sacrifice.'

Her forehead wrinkles. 'Huh?'

I look at her innocence and feel my heart crack right down the middle, adding yet another guilty fissure to that already-lined muscle. 'Love conquers all; a proverb that's on cue, for you may prove this old adage is true.'

Delia blinks at me with those dark eyes, and I want to reach out to her, but I can't let myself.

'Your family is trapped within a curse of anger and vengeance. You and one other have the power to break this curse once and for all.'

She swallows and then her eyes widen as what I said finally reaches her. 'But that's been going on for years. What sort of power could I possibly have to stop it?'

'The most powerful weapon that we, as humans, possess.' I smile. '*Love.* Both the ability to love others, and the ability to have others love us in return.'

'Love?' She speaks the word slowly, as if it has never before been naked on her tongue. 'I'm going to fall in love, *and* finally bring peace to my family? My town?'

I turn my face away; I can no longer bear to look at her.

'Just because you are prophesised to *end* this hatred, does not mean that you will *survive* it.'

'What are you saying?' asks Delia, squinting once again into the depths of the crystal ball. 'I don't understand what you are saying.'

I want to take her small hands in mine and feel their warmth, feel the beat of her blood beneath soft skin, feel the life that pulses there so effortlessly, but I keep my hands fisted in my lap. If I touch this girl, I know her skin will feel hard and cold, blue-hued, and as lifeless as a cut rose – still beautiful, yet dying before my eyes.

'Start looking for a way to change your path, Delia. Start looking before it is too late; I have foreseen your death, child, and it is not far away.'

She shakes her head, twitching it from side to side. Then she surges from the table so fast her chair thuds to the floor. It crashes with the last double-beat of a dying heart: *lub dub.*

In her hurry to escape my world – where the future becomes the now – she bumps the table with her hip and the crystal ball rolls towards the edge. It hangs there for just a second, as if perhaps gravity can be as easily thwarted as fate, and then it falls.

As the ball drops, and the beaded curtain draws a line between Delia and me once again, I pray for my crystal to crack open when it hits the floor, I pray for the prophecy to be freed, I pray for poor Delia to be liberated of the fate I've foreseen.

But my crystal ball does not break. It simply bounces, unharmed, unaltered, and rolls back to me, stopping at my bare toes.

chapter one

Orlando Starre is perched on a lookout, facing a cliff, towards which he is about to drive as fast as he can without stopping.

Well, unless Claude Rose stops first.

But Claude Rose *never* stops first.

Orlando tightens his hands until they cramp: one on the wheel, one on the gearshift. His foot ticks on the accelerator. A cold bead of sweat slides over his lip and into his mouth; the saltiness makes him think of blood, which makes him ask himself: what the hell am I doing?

He can't beat Claude at chicken. No one has *ever* beaten Claude at chicken. It's a wonder that idiot has not gone over the edge in pure stubborn refusal to brake first and lose dignity.

And it's not like the winner gets something substantial and worth risking his life for – like the other opponent's car for example. Nope. The winner gets the simple acknowledgement of being the winner. And who the hell really cares?

Well, Claude cares.

To Claude Rose, the acknowledgement of winning this stupid game is the most important thing in the world. Being unbeaten. Being number one. Being better than the Starres.

And as Orlando's fingers crunch tighter around the steering wheel, he sighs and admits that he cares about that, too. He wants to beat Claude. He wants to be number one. He wants to be better than the Roses.

His eyes flick towards Claude, who smiles towards the cliff edge, and something in that easy smile scares the absolute crap out of Orlando.

Claude is *relaxed*.

Claude has an acceptance of death.

Claude has never lost this challenge because he doesn't *care* if he goes over.

Claude doesn't care!

Oh, Jesus Christ, thinks Orlando.

His palms are slippery on the steering wheel now. He is about to lose. Or die. All because he tried to stop this very thing from happening in the first place. All because he put himself in between two workers of Rose Estate and Starre Wines, who'd been about to challenge each other. Again. Like they always seemed to be doing these days.

He'd lost count of how many times this week one of their vans returned with a crate of bottles all smashed after going up against a driver from Rose Estate. He'd lost count of how many times his father stood, red-cheeked and watery-eyed, staring at the sloshing van's interior, inside which his business ran down the drain. And he'd lost count of how many times his father had turned and beamed a proud smile at the loyal employees who'd refused to back down to the Roses.

Orlando wishes now he'd turned around the second he'd seen the two vans, engines growling at each other like wild beasts, waiting for the traffic lights to change.

He wishes he'd let them be the ones in this stupid position, facing the edge of a cliff.

He wishes he'd let them be the ones to receive the proud smile and watery eyes and clap on the back from his father.

But just once, just *once*, Orlando wants Morgan Starre to look at him that way.

The way Morgan always looks at Ben, Orlando's big brother

And so, when Claude had pulled up beside Orlando at those lights, well, he'd thought, wouldn't beating *Claude* be even better than beating the workers? Wouldn't beating the eldest of the two Rose children make his father even prouder?

'Don't tell me you're about to race the *workers*, Landy Boy?' Claude had sneered. 'Take me on, instead. First one to the lookout, last one to stop. Unless you're just a fairy boy, like your father?'

Even though he'd wanted to turn around, to just turn the hell around and go home, Orlando knew that the news of his cowardice would beat him there. That his father would stare at him, red-cheeked, and watery-eyed, and grimacing in shame.

Just like that, Orlando had stomped his foot on the accelerator, and squealed his car into this damn lookout seconds before Claude, and stared straight ahead at the 50 metres of road, and the eternity of nothing beyond it.

And he'd waited.

And now he is still waiting.

Waiting for whatever is about to happen.

Waiting to lose or to die.

Waiting for Claude's tyres to spin first, so Orlando might at least win *that* part of this stupid challenge.

But no. Seconds become minutes. More people gather, forming two distinct sides, cheering and beeping their horns in excitement and impatience at this true Rose versus Starre showdown.

Even over all the noise, Orlando still hears the pounding of waves against the rocks below. The ocean is angry today. Hungry. He wonders if his blood will soon churn and froth pink on the surface of the water.

When his door suddenly opens wide as a mouth, he squeals like a girl and almost slams the damn car into gear and flies towards the cliff edge.

Morgan Starre glares down, red-cheeked, and watery-eyed, and grimacing in shame.

Shame? Why? He'd done what his father would want him to do! He didn't back down to a Rose. He'd accepted the stupid challenge just like the beloved workers did all the time.

'Orlando Starre! What the hell are you doing?' Morgan rips the keys from the ignition. 'Are you trying to kill yourself?'

The crowd groans and boos as Orlando cringes out and stares at his feet and doesn't say all the words that bump around inside his brain: *I thought you'd be proud of me; I thought you'd be happy; I thought this is what a Starre is supposed to do. Why are you ashamed of me?*

'Hey, Morgan?'

Orlando glances up from beneath the dark hair that hides him away from the world, and sees Claude's parents, Shepherd and Imogen Rose, stomping toward them.

'Morgan!' Shepherd Rose yells again.

Orlando feels a surge of electricity zap through his father, who bristles and straightens to his full height. 'Shepherd,' he snarls, low and rumbling like a growl from a wolf's throat.

Beside Orlando, his mother straightens too, and she hisses to her husband, 'Go easy on them, love.'

'Your bloody son is a menace!' Morgan stabs a shaking finger in the direction of Claude. 'Organising these damn reckless races.'

'My son?' Shepherd Rose, white with anger, jerks his

arm away from his wife, who tries unsuccessfully to hold him back. 'My son? Claude says it was *your* son who gave out the challenge!'

The two men storm towards each other, and the crowd falls silent, rapt, gleeful. But Orlando's mother – black hair wild about her face – launches herself between the the two men, pushing against her husband's chest.

Morgan growls at his wife, 'Move, Desdemona!'

But she shakes her head. 'Morgan Starre, you will *not* take one more step towards him. You will *not* start a fight in the middle of this crowd!'

The *whoop-whoop* of a siren slices through the tension-thick air, and the group of onlookers parts down the middle. A police car slides through, a stroboscopic disco of blue and red flashing over every eager face, with the giant silhouette of Sergeant Burgundy hulking over the steering wheel.

Orlando closes his eyes and groans as the officer steps out of the cruiser and rises to his full height, staring down first at Morgan Starre, and then Shepherd Rose. 'You two will not learn, will you?' he shouts. 'You won't be satisfied until this hatred is quenched by your own blood!' Burgundy flashes his brown eyes at Orlando. 'Or your *children's* blood! This is the *third* time this week that you, or your children, or your employees, have caused some kind of disturbance! I'm giving you one more chance.' He holds up a stubby finger. '*One.* The very next one of you who disturbs the quiet of my streets will be arrested and sent straight to jail. No trial. No bail.' He turns to Shepherd Rose. 'Rose, follow me now to the courthouse, and Starre, you come this afternoon. We *will* get this mess sorted out once and for all.'

Burgundy glances at each of them, one by one, his piercing eyes lingering, then he turns and shouts to the crowd. 'As for the rest of you, get out of here before I start giving out fines!' Then he folds himself back into his cruiser and drives away.

After a long and silent glare at Shepherd, Morgan turns and pinches the back of Orlando's neck, leading him to his car. 'Who *did* start it this time?'

'Not me!'

Morgan raises his eyebrows.

'It wasn't!' Orlando clears his throat. 'I was trying to *stop* a race breaking out between the two delivery vans, and then Claude came along. He called me a ...' He looks down at his fidgeting hands because he can't stand to look at his father's eyes anymore. 'Never mind.'

His father grunts, and Orlando can't tell if it's a proud grunt at his refusal to back down to a Rose, or a frustrated grunt at this refusal to back down to a Rose.

'Oh, where's Ben?' Desdemona sighs and stares at the clouds beyond the cliff edge. 'Have you seen him today? I'm so glad he wasn't involved in all of this.'

And there it is. That twinge in Orlando's gut that always accompanies a conversation about Ben: the golden boy, the favourite son. Poor depressed Ben. Poor sensitive

Ben. Poor perfect Ben! Never mind that Orlando had almost driven his car over a cliff, just so long as poor effing Ben didn't have to witness it!

'I saw him earlier,' Orlando tells her, 'walking among that grove of trees at the edge of town.'

Reflected in his mother's dark eyes, Orlando sees her thoughts flash on those trees, and their thick sturdy branches, and their perfection for attaching a noosed rope.

'He looked okay,' Orlando says, touching his mother's arm. 'He looked like he wanted to be alone, so I left him to it.'

Morgan nods at her. 'He's been so down lately. More than usual, I mean. He stays out all night long, then stumbles home and draws all the curtains to make an artificial night. I'm worried. Unless something changes soon, this mood of his … well, it can only lead to trouble.'

There's silence. Orlando can feel them waiting for him to ask, but he doesn't want to ask, because frankly he doesn't want to know the answer. It's not that he doesn't *care* about Ben, or his problems, and it's not that he doesn't want to help. He just wants his parents to interact with him because they truly care about *him*, about what might be going on in *his* life, and not because they want him to help poor precious Ben get through yet another life crisis.

But eventually, as he always does, Orlando sighs. 'What's his problem this time?'

Morgan shrugs. 'He won't talk to anyone!'

Just then, as if drawn by the mere mention of his beloved name, Ben Starre speeds past the lookout, heading into town.

Orlando snatches up his keys – along with this opportunity to get away from his parents – and slides into his car. 'Leave him to me.'

In the rear-view mirror, Orlando watches his parents watching him, and he can see hope blooming pink in their cheeks. Shifting his focus to the reflection of his own eyes, and to the hope that is also visible there, he wonders exactly what outcome he is hoping for.

chapter two

The tattooist is not what Ben Starre expects to see when he enters the studio. Puny with orange hair, freckled skin, thick-lensed glasses, and a cute cartoon Pegasus tattoo on his skinny shoulder.

Where is the big, scary, ink-covered, biker-type? Ben wonders. Although, if the photos on the walls are anything to go by, this tiny dweeb can certainly draw.

'You're wondering what a guy like me is doing in a place like this, aren't you?' The artist has a high, girlish voice, and his R's sound like W's.

'What? No, of course not!' Ben stammers.

'Yes, you are, and it's cool; that's what everyone thinks when they first see me in here.'

Shrugging, then smiling, Ben slaps a creased napkin down on the glass-topped bench. Drawn roughly in smudged ink is a banner-wrapped heart with a single name in the middle: *Olivia.* 'Could you stick this on me?'

The tattooist smooths over the napkin and nods. 'Sure. Just give me a jiffer to draw up a stencil.'

A *jiffer*?

Ben smiles and sits on a leather chair to wait, just as a familiar car pulls up outside.

The bell above the door announces the entrance of his younger brother, his dark curls bouncing with every strutting step.

What's he looking so pleased about? Ben wonders as Orlando beams at him.

'Morning, bro!'

'Morning?' Ben groans. 'You mean it's not even *noon* yet?'

Orlando looks up at the clock on the wall. 'It's only nine o'clock.'

'Oh, man, is that all?' He shakes his head. 'Sad hours seem long.'

'What sadness could possibly slow down the hours of the *wonderful* Ben Starre?'

'Well ...' He shrugs and roll his eyes. 'Not having the thing that makes time speed up. Obviously.'

'Oh, no.' Orlando grunts himself up onto a bench. 'Are you in love *again*?'

Why is he here? Ben wonders. Why can't he just leave me alone? He shakes his head and says, 'Out.'

'*Out* of love?' Orlando frowns.

'She doesn't love me, okay!'

'Why is it always about *love* with you? Why can't you just go around screwing them instead?'

'Because, Casanova, I'm not like you!' Ben sighs. 'Can we just drop it, please?'

Orlando holds up his hands. 'Sure, man, sure.'

The tattooist walks into the room again, pressing a stencil against Ben's upper arm and then peels it away, imprinting a purple outline on the skin.

Ben holds back a laugh as Orlando raises his eyebrows.

'Ready?' asks the tattooist.

Ben nods.

The tattooist clicks on the tattoo gun, and the needles hum.

Gritting his teeth through a surge of pain, Ben mutters, 'Why do you look all puffed up and shiny today, anyway?'

Orlando's eyes flash brightly, and Ben looks away before he goes blind.

'No, don't tell me,' says Ben, realising the answer. 'I've heard it all before. This stupid Starre-Rose rivalry; they think it's all about hate, but it's really about *love*. They've got it all upside-down: hateful love, loving hate, sad happiness! Stupid. It's enough to make you laugh.' And he tries to laugh, but can't find the sound inside him, because really, it's *not* funny. None of it is.

'No,' says Orlando, 'it's enough to make you cry.'

Surprised, Ben looks up at his little brother. Does he get it? Does he finally get it?

'What is?' Ben asks him.

'You and your damn sadness!' Orlando says. 'You're making everyone around you depressed.'

'Well,' Ben shrugs, 'that's love. And if it's too depressing for you to be near me, go away! I have enough to worry about.'

'Nah, let me hang here with you.'

'Why? I'm not myself today; this is not the real Ben Starre, he's off somewhere else.'

Orlando jumps down off the counter and squints over the tattooist's shoulder at the black letters oozing blood from Ben's arm. 'Olivia?' He sighs. 'Okay, spill: who is she?'

'The most beautiful girl in town, that's who.'

'So what's the deal? She have another guy?'

Ben presses his lips and looks away. 'Not exactly.'

'Well, what then?' asks Orlando.

'A girl,' Ben mumbles.

'Huh?'

'She has a *girlfriend*, okay! She's *gay*.'

Orlando grins. 'Sweet.'

Ben shakes his head at the unfairness of it all. 'Such a waste: beauty like that. It will die with her! Won't bless future generations. There should be laws about beautiful people and procreation.'

'She *might* have kids? Gay people can do that these days, you know.'

'Not helping, Orlando.'

'Sorry. Listen, just forget about her.'

'Oh, yeah, okay. That's *super* advice! I don't know why I didn't think of that!' Ben rolls his eyes at his idiot brother. 'And how exactly do I do that, genius?'

'Well, look around you for starters!' Orlando points out the front window as three women in tight singlets and denim shorts bounce past.

'That only makes me think of her *more*! A man suddenly blinded can never forget his lost eyesight. Thanks anyway, but just forget it, okay?'

'No, I won't forget it. On the contrary, I'm going to *help* you forget it!'

'Lucky me.'

'I'm serious,' says Orlando. 'You just need to find another chick and you'll feel better. It's like when you have a headache and someone stomps on your foot; you don't feel the headache anymore.'

'I'll give *you* a headache,' Ben mumbles. What the hell is his deal, anyway? Why the sudden brotherly affection? Probably just wants to get laid, himself. Well, too bad. I'm not helping him ball around.

Orlando squints his eyes. 'You mad at me?'

'No,' Ben sighs and reminds himself that it isn't Orlando's fault. 'I'm not mad,' he says. 'I just feel like I'm *going* mad; driven crazy with heartache and the pang of unrequited love.'

Orlando blinks as if he actually knows what this feels like, and Ben frowns, and is about to ask, but then the tattooist looks up from his work.

'You two going to the Rose Estate celebration tonight?'

As one, the brothers snort out a laugh.

'Uh ... I don't think *we* are invited,' says Orlando.

'It's none of my business,' the tattooist smiles, slowly, 'but I happen to know that a Miss Olivia will be there.'

At the sound of her name, that name, the only name there is, Ben's stomach clenches itself around his heart. 'Really? You know her?'

The tattooist nods. 'She's a wine critic. The party is to launch the Rose's new wine. It starts at eight tonight, at the Rose Estate. You guys should go. If you're not Starres, that is.' He laughs and bends back over his work.

Ben and Orlando raise their eyebrows at each other.

'Well, what do you think?' Orlando asks and his black eyes shine. '*She's* going to be there, as well as a bevy of other beautiful broads!'

'Are you serious, man?'

Orlando sighs. 'You don't get it, do you? It's the perfect place to compare her so-called beauty to all the others. Might make you realise that Olivia is not that great after all! You'll forget about her,' Orlando clicks his fingers, 'just like that!'

'No.' Ben shakes his head. 'The sun has never seen anyone more beautiful than Olivia since the beginning of the world! So if my eyes ever *do* find someone more beautiful, I hope they burst into flames!'

Orlando frowns. 'You hope who burst into flames? The beautiful women?'

'No, you idiot, my eyes. Don't worry about it, I was trying to be poetic.'

Orlando smiles. 'You know Ross is the only one who understands your stupid way of speaking. Hey, do you think he'll come with me? I mean us?'

'I don't know, man ...'

Orlando leans forward. 'You don't think Ross will come?'

'I mean,' says Ben, 'I don't know if *I* should come.'

'Come on, bro. I need you. Will you crash a party with me?'

Orlando's face is open wide, and for a second Ben sees the little kid who used to waddle around after him, imitating his every move, and irritating him because of it, yet flattering him at the same time. He is Orlando's brother. His big brother. This kid looks up to him, right? And so Ben gives a long sigh. 'Do I have a choice?'

'Nope!'

'Well, what did you ask me for, then? Yes, little brother, I will accompany you.'

Orlando grins, and, surprised at himself, Ben grins as well.

'Anyway,' Ben looks down at his arm, 'I'll be able to show Olivia what I've done for her.'

'And what?' asks Orlando. 'You think carving her name into your flesh with ink is going to magically make her want cock? Sorry, man, but it ain't gonna happen. Trust me, I'm going to help you forget this chick, or die trying!'

chapter three

Shepherd Rose watches his neighbour, Guy Shylock, nodding along to the story; his elbows rest on the desk, his head propped in his hands, his eyes wide and enthusiastic as a toddler's at a magic show.

'So, when I got to the courthouse,' Shepherd tells him, 'Burgundy made me sign a contract that prevents Starres and Roses from *knowingly being within a hundred metres of each other*. Morgan Starre will have to sign it this afternoon. It shouldn't be hard for two grown men to keep the peace. Anyway, *we're* not the problem. Not anymore. Half the time these brawls have nothing to do with us; we aren't drag-racing down every damn street, and toward cliffs, are we?'

Shepherd thinks of Claude, and his jaw sets. He hopes this new law will stop his son from acting like a lunatic and almost killing himself on a daily basis.

'It's a pity you and Morgan Starre have been enemies

for so long, Mr Rose,' says Guy. 'What happened anyway? I heard you used to be friends.'

Shepherd's eyes dart to the photo frame on his desk, inside which Imogen, Claude and Delia – frozen in time – smile up at him.

'I beat Morgan Starre at tennis once,' says Shepherd. 'What can I say? He's a sore loser.'

Standing from his chair, Shepherd paces the floor of the den, stopping every few seconds to glance at his neighbour – this young man in a ridiculous T-shirt with a black printed bowtie and matching cummerbund. His black hair is cut short, neat around the ears; his friendly brown eyes follow Shepherd around the room like a puppy. 'And please, I've told you a hundred times to call me *Shepherd*, not Mr Rose.'

'Sorry, Mr … Shepherd.' Guy smiles. 'So, is Delia glad to be home?'

'Oh … Um … Yes, I assume so.' Shepherd looks down again at the photo frame. 'Two years away is a long time.'

'*Three* years.'

'Hmm?'

'She's been gone *three* years,' says Guy.

'Oh.' He nods. 'Of course.'

'You must be so proud, seeing her graduate with honours!'

'Yes … Right.'

'When is she planning on taking up the reins of Rose Estate, then?'

'Not sure exactly. She said something about a gap year.'

'I can understand that.' Guy nods. 'After I graduated, I wanted some wind-down time before entering the real world, you know? Before becoming an official responsible adult.'

'Yes,' says Shepherd. 'Responsible.'

'Are you okay?' Guy asks. 'You seem ... distracted.'

'Listen, Guy.' Shepherd clears his throat. 'I guess you know why I called you here. It's about the money I owe you.'

'Yes, that was some game last night, wasn't it?' says Guy. 'You just couldn't seem to get a good firm grip of Lady Luck's arse!'

'Lady Luck's arse?' Shepherd wonders how the hell he could have sunk so low as to be sucking up to this innocent little bastard. Clearing his throat, Shepherd closes his eyes and listens to the words that he wishes he were not speaking. 'You see, Guy, the thing is, I don't actually have the money on me. It's all tied up in the company: the vineyard, land, produce, machinery, that sort of thing. You understand? Don't get me wrong,' he rushes on, 'I'm good for it, I am, just not all in one go, that's all.'

Guy tips his head to the side, and suddenly he no longer looks like the twenty-something-year-old who was lucky enough to be born wealthy. He doesn't know what it's like to work your fingers to the bone, to build an empire from the very dirt. He doesn't know what it's like to take risks. He doesn't know what it's like to lose. The spoilt little son of a bitch doesn't know how God damned lucky he is.

'I'll tell you what, Mr ... Shepherd, because I like you, I have a proposition for you.'

Shepherd sighs. 'Name your price, son?'

'Delia.'

He frowns. 'What about her?'

'I want her.'

'What do you mean: you *want* her? You want to employ her?'

'I want to *date* her.'

'What?' Shepherd's jaw falls.

'Just think,' says Guy. 'If Delia and I end up getting married, we could combine our properties. You'd make double the profits, and I'd have a beautiful wife, a family to raise one day. Think about it. Also, you would be my father-in-law, and I don't take money from family.' He leans back in his chair. 'Your debt will disappear.'

Jesus. Maybe this kid isn't so innocent after all.

'The whole thing?' Shepherd asks. 'Just wiped clean?'

'The whole thing.'

Jesus Christ! Sweat prickles the skin of Shepherd's upper lip, and he licks it off. It tastes like salt and chance and opportunity.

'This is the twenty-first century, Guy; fathers don't *choose* who their daughters will date, or marry!'

'I know that ... but ... could you just *ask* her?' sighs Guy. 'Set us up or something?'

Shepherd bites his bottom lip. He knows Delia would never agree to being set up; she's too damn stubborn. She's too much like him. Ironically.

'Please?'

Christ. He runs a hand through his white hair. He could more easily give Guy a pound of his own flesh than a date with his daughter, but the look on that poor kid's face is too shiny and hopeful to smear with disappointment. And, let's face it, the future possibility is a very tempting one. 'You're coming to the wine launch tonight, aren't you?'

'Of course,' Guy says. 'I wouldn't miss it for the world.'

'Ask her for a dance and take it from there,' Shepherd says, 'but I can't promise you anything!'

Pulling his handkerchief out, Shepherd blots more sweat from his brow and prays that his daughter will allow herself to be wooed by the boy next door. He prays that his crushing debt will remain a secret from his wife. He prays that the bank will not rip his home and business out from underneath his feet.

He looks at this grinning kid, this God damned son of a bitch, this businessman to whom he's just essentially sold his only daughter, and Shepherd Rose prays for a God damn miracle.

chapter four

'Do you know who's going to be at this party tonight?' Delia asks.

'No.' Katherine turns from the mirror. 'Who?'

'I don't know, that's why I was asking you.'

'How would I know?' Katherine shrugs. 'It's *your* party?'

'Because,' Delia says, 'you know things in this town.'

'Well, I know that neighbour of yours is gorgeous! I just met him downstairs. I hope *he's* coming.' Katherine's mouth purses in a stiff oval as she applies bright red lipstick. 'Anyway, I wish you'd get yourself out into the world and *look* for him already, instead of waiting for him to come to you.' She smacks her lips together.

'Look for who?' Delia asks.

'You know very well who!' says Katherine. 'You're always going on about true love, and soul mates, and all that crap, but you have to make your own fate.'

'Fate?' Delia sucks in a breath at her friend's words

and the image of my crystal ball rises in her memory like a moon. She hadn't even told her about me yet, or the prophecy I had given her. She looks at Katherine and shrugs. 'Fate is already predetermined. No matter what I do, my life will turn out the way it has been written.'

'But, what if it's written,' Katherine says, 'that you're supposed to get out there and *look* for your soul mate, and by sitting around waiting for him, you'll never find him.'

'Well,' says Delia, 'what if it's written that when I find him, we'll fall desperately in love and end up killing ourselves over it!'

'What?' Katherine frowns her perfectly shaped eyebrows.

'Wouldn't it be better, then, if I *never* meet him?'

'Delia, that's just dumb. You have to stop making excuses. I mean, come on; you've never even had a real boyfriend!'

'Why waste time dating men who aren't my destiny?'

'Because it's *fun*! I think you're just too picky.'

'No I'm not,' says Delia, joining Katherine at the dressing table and digging through the top drawer for mascara. 'You're the picky one.'

'At least I give a guy a chance before I dump him.'

'I give chances!'

'Yeah? Okay, tell me again what was wrong with all those college guys: Nick Weaver?'

'He thought he was better than everyone at everything!' Delia says. 'He was such an ass.'

'Peter Carpenter?'

'Too nervous; never spoke up for himself.'

'Francis Bellows?'

'Too feminine. He had that high, squeaky voice.'

'Rob Tailor?'

'Too pale. He was like a moonbeam.'

'Tom Tinker?'

'Dense. It was like talking to a brick wall.'

'Snug Joiner?'

'He had that loud, roaring voice, remember? Scary. And his name was *Snug*. I mean, come on!'

'No, you're not picky at all!' laughs Katherine. 'You know what I think?'

'No,' Delia sighs, 'but I'm sure you're going to tell me.'

'I think you're scared.'

'Of what?'

'Of rejection. Of being hurt. You fault them before they can fault you. You push guys away.'

Delia crosses her arms. 'So do you!'

'Well, if I do it's because they try to change who I am. I'm a shrew who refuses to be tamed by anyone thank you! You, on the other hand, push them away before you even know if they're worth *not* pushing away!'

'None of them was my soul mate.'

'But, how do you *know?*'

'Because,' says Delia, 'I shouldn't have to give my soul mate a chance; I'll know instantly. And there was nothing *instant* about any of those guys. If we're supposed to be together, then fate will make it happen.' She looks away from her friend. 'There's nothing I can do to change that, either way.'

'Okay.' Katherine stares at Delia. 'What's up with you tonight? You're being weird. Like, weirder than normal.'

'Nothing.'

'Delia! It's me. Spill.'

'No.' Delia shakes her head. 'You'll think I'm nuts.'

'Like I don't already? Come on. Tell me.'

In one long sigh, Delia exhales her words. 'I saw a psychic this morning, and I'm going to fall in love, and end my family's feud, and then kill myself.'

'Wow.' Katherine drops onto the edge of the bed and leans forward. 'That's dead spooky.'

'Tell me about it.' Delia's arms cross over her chest, hugging herself as if against a cool wind.

'Because,' continues Katherine, 'I just found out that I got the lead part in *Romeo and Juliet*!'

'What?' Delia blinks at her friend.

'I'm Juliet!' she squeals.

'That's great,' Delia says slowly, 'but we're talking about *me* now, remember?'

Katherine stands, and with gesticulating hands, she begins to speak in a terrible British accent. 'Two households, both alike in dignity, in fair Verona where we lay our scene. From ancient grudge, break to new mutiny, where civil blood makes civil hands unclean. From forth the fatal loins of these two foes, a pair of star-crossed lovers take their life!' Katherine grins. 'Whose misadventured piteous overthrows doth, with their death, bury their parents' strife!'

Delia rolls her eyes. 'Again, can we please focus on me for just a sec?'

'It's Shakespeare,' Katherine says.

'Yes, I am aware who wrote your starring role. But I'm kind of having a New Age crisis here: I was just told I am going to *die*.'

'Did it sound familiar?'

'What?'

'The line!' Katherine's eyes widen, as if they can somehow convey the severity of whatever the hell she is blabbing on about.

Pinching the bridge of her nose, Delia sighs. 'It may have, if I'd been able to understand a word of it!'

'You're not going to die, Delia. That fortune-teller ripped you off. What she told you was basically the storyline of *Romeo and Juliet*!'

'Really?'

'Truly.'

'Huh. Damn it!' Delia smiles. 'That means I'm not going to meet *him* tonight then.'

'Well, if you do, just promise me that you won't end up drinking a sleeping potion to fake your death, because – spoiler alert – the plan backfires.'

'I'll try to remember that.'

'I wonder what happened, though,' says Katherine,

'between your folks and the Starres, I mean. The Starres must have done something pretty horrible to your parents for Mr R hold a grudge against them; your dad always seems so tolerant of everybody.'

'I don't know.' Delia shrugs. 'They never talk about it. I met Morgan Starre once,' she says, remembering the way he had patted her on the head in the supermarket when she was just a girl. She'd been there with her mum, and Morgan had smiled and said she was a beautiful child. 'He seemed fine to me.'

'But, Morgan Starre *is* your father's enemy, right? So who would you choose as your Romeo? Orlando or Ben?'

'God, I don't know, Katherine; I never met them. My parents made sure of that.'

'Well, Ben is totally gorgeous, but Orlando is quite the ladies' man.' Katherine raises her eyebrows and grins. 'If you know what I mean.'

'Then he'd be perfect for *you*, wouldn't he!'

'You're no fun!' Katherine sighs. 'Anyway, how do I look?'

'Isn't your dress a little ... small?'

'Not small, honey. *Fitting!*' says Katherine, turning her head to check herself from behind. 'There's a very fine difference. Something that you would do well to learn.'

'Why? What's wrong with this?' Delia nudges Katherine out of the way so she can see her own dress in the mirror. It flows over her body in pretty folds of fabric, and she doesn't know what Katherine is talking about: this dress looks fantastic.

There is a soft tap on the door, and Delia turns to see her mother, seeming lost in the frame of the doorway. Imogen Rose is a tiny bird of a woman. Her thin bones look fragile beneath her papery skin; Delia often wonders how her mother could ever have given birth to her, let alone someone as solid and forceful as Claude. How had the woman not shattered beneath the weight of her pregnancies?

'Hi, girls,' Imogen says, in her thin voice. 'Nearly ready? The guests will be arriving any minute now.'

'Yep.' Delia smiles at her. 'We're all set.'

Imogen hops across the room and perches like a sparrow on the edge of Delia's bed. 'Uh, Delia, can I have a word?'

'Of course.'

'Is this private?' asks Katherine. 'Family business? Do you want me to leave? Because I can leave, I don't mind, I won't be offended or anything, Mrs R.'

Imogen hesitates, chewing on her lip for a moment, and staring at Katherine. 'No, that's okay,' she says, then faces Delia again. 'Honey, you know young Guy Shylock from next door?'

Katherine sits up straighter.

'The one who owns the orange orchard?' says Delia. 'Yes, of course. He seems sweet.'

'He seems sexy!' says Katherine. 'Now he's the type of guy I could see myself marrying!'

'Actually,' says my mother, 'it's funny you should mention that.'

'What: me being married?' Katherine frowns. 'I don't really see how that's at all funny! As soon as a man gets a ring on your finger, he tries to mould you into his dream woman! See, that's why Guy would be perfect for me; he doesn't seem the type. I'll tell you this right now though; no man will ever make me change, no way! None of that, "Jump!" "How high?" stuff for me. Tell it like it is. If it's night, I'll say it's night. If it's day, I'll say it's day. And I'll never say it's day, if it's really night, just because my husband tells me to! You know what I mean?'

Imogen clears her throat, and Delia holds back a laugh.

'Oh, I'm sorry, Mrs R; you came in here with something to say to Delia and here I am, talking away like there's no tomorrow! Talk! Talk! Talk! But I'll shut up now.' Katherine mimes locking her lips shut with an invisible key that she then throws away over her shoulder. 'See? Shutting up. Oops! Sorry!' She clamps her mouth shut again. 'Starting now. I mean now. Now.'

'I was just wondering,' Imogen says, sighing and turning her attention back to Delia, 'how you feel about marriage?'

'Is this another one of those "I'll love you no matter

what" talks?' Delia asks. 'Because I've already told you: I'm not gay.'

'No, honey, I'm just curious.'

The look on her mother's face seems deeper than simple curiosity, which makes Delia curious about her curiosity. 'Getting married is an honour.' Delia shrugs, and then adds, 'I guess.'

And Imogen smiles, seemingly happy with that response.

'I mean,' Delia continues, suddenly feeling a little nervous, 'it's an honour if you find the right person.'

'But, sweetheart,' Imogen places a hand on Delia's shoulder, 'you're not even *looking* for the right person.'

Katherine opens her mouth, but seeing the look on Delia's face, shuts it, and pretends to lock her lips again.

'By the time I was your age,' says Imogen, 'I was already married, had your brother and was pregnant with you!'

'Yes, and I'm sure you and Dad were just thrilled about that.'

'What is that supposed to mean?' Imogen laughs and looks away from Delia's gaze. 'Of *course* we were thrilled!'

'I'm not *you*, Mum. You were lucky, you found your soul mate by the time you were my age; but, I'm still looking. Why is that such a crime? Why can't I believe in love at first sight? You do!'

'Because,' says Imogen, 'it doesn't always work that way.'

'Don't waste your breath, Mrs R, I already gave her this lecture,' says Katherine.

'I'll *know* him.' Delia stares at both of them. 'When I meet my *one*, I'll know. Just like you did with Dad.'

'Well,' Imogen smiles. '*Guy* would very much like to be your *one*.'

'What?' says Katherine, her mouth dropping.

'He spoke to your father about it earlier.'

'The good ones always want *you*!' Katherine walks back over to the dressing table and re-applies her lipstick. 'You're so lucky! Guy Freaking Shylock wants you! He has a perfect body, like an artist sculpted it from granite! Those pecs, and that bum! Oh!'

'Katherine!' Delia laughs.

'Please, take him,' she says. 'You'll only throw him out after five minutes anyway, and then I can be there to comfort him.'

'That's harsh,' Delia says.

'But it's true.'

'Delia?' Imogen leans forward and takes Delia's hand. 'What do you say? Could you give Guy a shot? He'll be at the party tonight. All this man lacks to make him perfect and complete,' she touches Delia's cheek, 'is a *bride*.'

'God, Mum, you're so old fashioned! I've only been home two days, and you're already trying to set me up! I'll *see*.' She sighs. 'If he is likable, I'll try to like him. But if he isn't the one I'm supposed to marry, I won't waste any more time on him.'

'And then I can have him!' adds Katherine.

'Girls!' The booming voice of Shepherd Rose floats up the stairs. 'People are arriving!'

'We'll be right down!' Imogen calls back. She stands up and pulls Delia to her feet. 'Okay, Delia, Guy is waiting!' She claps her hands and practically skips out of the room.

'She just loves playing match-maker, doesn't she?' Delia tries to laugh, but the anxiety in her stomach grips too hard and suddenly she almost wants to cry.

'Come on.' Katherine slaps Delia on the bum as she sashays out of the bedroom. 'Seek happy nights to happy days!'

'What?' asks Delia, following her through the door.

'It's Shakespeare!'

'Oh,' Delia smiles and shakes her head. 'Of course it is.'

chapter five

The moon hangs full and low in the sky, glowing orange, and shining an eerie spotlight on the heads of Orlando Starre, and Ross Aylind, who both bounce down the moonlit street, buoyed by the mere promise of frivolity. Ben though, is not very buoyant tonight. His mind is so weighed down by melancholy, it seeps right into his shoes; his feet drag and trip him up every few steps.

'And anyway,' he calls ahead, 'how the hell are we getting in here?'

Orlando looks back over his shoulder and gives a full-mouth grin. 'Relax, will you?' From a small satchel slung over his shoulder, he pulls out a black wig and a fake beard.

'Seriously?' says Ben. 'You don't honestly believe this is going to work?'

'Sure it will!' Orlando says. 'We'll sneak in, have a bit of fun, pick up some hot chicks, and – once you realise that there *is* life beyond the fair Olivia – we'll take said hot chicks home and ...'

'I told you, I'm not taking anyone home,' says Ben.

'Oh, Benny! You have to pick up.' Ross snatches one of the wigs, fits it on his head, and spins around. The hair fans out around him.

'I can't.' Ben shakes his head. 'I'm too heavy with rejection to pick up *anything*. It pins me to the ground and I can't move. Who would want to be with ...' He looks down at himself. 'With *this*.' And then he looks at Ross. 'Apart from *you*, I mean.'

'Nuh-uh! I got over you a long time ago, Ben Starre,' says Ross. 'Besides, you're a lover!' he cries. 'A hopeless romantic. If you're pinned down and feel too heavy to walk, just borrow wings from your friend, Cupid, and fly up again!'

Ben narrows his eyes. 'Cupid? That son of a bitch's arrow stabbed me in the heart. I'm bleeding to death, here! I *can't* fly.' Then he trips and stumbles and falls on his knees. 'Ouch! See? Love's a bitch.'

Ross offers him a hand up. 'I have an idea.' He puts his arms around Ben's neck and leans in until his lips are just a breath away and Ben feels the heat of Ross all up his body.

Ben clears his throat and thinks about how long it's been since anyone was this close to him.

'If love is a bitch to you ...' Ross whispers, sliding his

hot hand down Ben's back until his fingertips sneak into the waistband of Ben's jeans.

'Dude, stop it, will you?'

'Then, why don't you ...' Ross continues to breathe words in Ben's ear. 'Be a bastard to love?' And he jumps away, laughing, and leaving Ben cold in the sudden absence of body heat.

'Cock tease!' Ben mutters, but he smiles.

Ross laughs and blows him a kiss. 'If you hurt love for hurting you, you'll beat it! You'll win.'

'Hurt love?' Ben says. 'What does that even mean?'

'Now you know how I feel,' Orlando laughs, 'when *you* start talking all poetic and making no sense!'

'Really?' Ben raises his eyebrows. 'I sound as bad as *that*? Gee, man, I'm really sorry!'

'Well, I'm no expert,' says Orlando, 'but I believe that what the charming Ross is saying is ...'

'Ah, shucks,' says Ross. 'You think I'm *charming*, Lan?'

Orlando clears his throat and keeps speaking. 'Is that you need a night of meaningless, animalistic, no-love-allowed sex! And by doing so, you will prove to love that you don't need it after all.'

'See?' Ross nods. 'Lan gets me.'

Ben closes his eyes and imagines a nameless girl lying naked in his bed while he kisses his way down her exquisite body. He has to admit, it's a nice thought. Until, in his imagination, Ben looks up from between her legs just as a beam of moonlight falls across her face, and he sees that she is, in fact, Olivia. And then she starts laughing, rolls off the bed, and runs from the room, leaving Ben once again heavy with a desire that he knows will never be fulfilled, and a love that will be forever unrequited.

He sighs as they all stop in the shadows before the Roses' driveway and, while staring up at the intricate, wrought iron gates, they don the wigs and fake beards.

Around them, the darkness is heavy with music and flavour and laughter. The soft, unmistakable clink of crystal against crystal dances out and tickles Ben beneath his chin, beckoning him forward.

Maybe this could be fun after all, he thinks.

'Now, remember,' says Ross, turning to face Ben, 'as soon as we get in, find yourself a pretty girl, or boy, I won't judge.'

'The drunker, the better!' adds Orlando.

'We won't have much time,' says Ross. 'As soon as either of you boys are recognised, it's over. So, come on, we're wasting daylight!'

'No we're not; it's night time,' Ben mumbles.

Ross sighs. 'I meant: we're wasting *time*, which is *like* wasting sunshine during the day.' He taps a finger against Ben's forehead. 'Use your brains to work out what I mean, instead of trying to be clever!'

Ben steps away. 'I don't know if this is such a good idea.'

'And why not?' asks Ross.

'I uh ... I went to a fortune teller this afternoon.' The words are out before Ben can stop them, and his face burns. He hadn't planned on telling anyone about me, about what I had told him, about what I had warned him was coming, but Ross has always had this strange power over Ben; he could never keep anything secret from him. Especially fear.

'You mean, Mab?' Ross says, his eyes brightening. 'The one at the carnival? So did I.'

'Really?' Ben gapes. 'What did she tell you?'

'That gypsies often lie,' says Ross.

Ross thinks I am a fraud. And for a second, I know that Ben feels liberated by this notion. Enlightened that he could be freed of my prophecy so easily. But then, I see Ben's eyes cloud as he thinks about me. He really thinks about me, and what I said, and I know that Ben Starre does *not* think I am a fake. He does *not* agree with Ross. Ben believes that the only lying I have done is to lie in bed and see glimpses the future.

His future.

'Oh, no.' Ross frowns, and then he sighs. 'She got in there, didn't she?'

'Well,' Ben shrugs. 'She got some stuff right. It was spooky.'

'That's what she *does*! She reads people. She goes on reactions; feels around until she thinks she's hit a weak spot, then she milks you for all you're worth!' Ross shakes his head. 'She's like a fairy! She shrinks herself to the size of a ... a ...' Looking down at his hands, at the tiny silver ring with its delicate striped orange stone, he holds his hand out to Ben. 'An agate stone! She rides in a magical chariot made out of an empty hazelnut shell. A small, grey-coated gnat is her driver, and with a crop made from a cricket's bone he whips the tiny microscopic creatures harnessed to the carriage by spider webs and moonbeams!'

'You're crazy,' Ben mutters, but he smiles at his friend.

'In this carriage,' says Ross, 'Mab is drawn into your mind, the mind of a *lover*, and there she foretells of *love!*' he yells the word, throwing his arms wide. 'But she plagues this promise of love with blistered paranoia! She weaves it through your thoughts like the thinnest threads of gossamer, and in these threads she traps you, like a fly in a web! You start seeing omens everywhere. You start believing that misfortune is coming for you and, in thinking this way, you walk straight into Miss Fortune's trap!'

Ross grabs Ben's shoulders. 'It doesn't matter what she tells you, if you believe in the *possibility* of it being fulfilled, then it *will* be fulfilled. If you believe something is going to happen, then you will ultimately cause it to happen; subconsciously you will *make it come true!*'

Ross's words cause my breath to halt in my throat as I watch and I wait to see how Ben will react.

'Calm down, Ross!' Ben shrugs him away. 'Calm

down. You don't know what you're talking about; you weren't there.'

'Fortune telling is nothing but silly imagination,' Ross says, backing away from Ben. His voice is soft again, whispering. 'Prophecy, destiny, fate: they're the children of idle brains, born from vain fantasy, as thin as air, and less predictable than the wind.'

Orlando steps between Ben and Ross, frowning at them both. 'Did this crazy Mab woman predict that we would be late for this damn party? Cos if she did, then I'm a believer! The meals are already over; people will be leaving soon. Let's go!'

Fixing his fake beard, and taking Ross's hand, Orlando pulls him forward through the gates and into the lights that twinkle all along the driveway like a path made of stars.

Ben steps back into the shadows and watches them both glowing with a combined longing for fun. Just as he is about to step out into the light himself, he hears my throaty voice whisper in his memory.

'*You carry a prophecy.*'

Something cold throbs heavy in his chest, in his gut, and he is once again pinned to the spot. But this time, it is not his sadness that holds him in place, but a sense of self preservation. Because it is going to happen tonight. He knows this more certainly than he has ever known anything. It will be tonight. And there is absolutely nothing he can do to change it.

Just walk away, he tells himself. Just turn and leave and don't even glance back.

But he knows it will make no difference. This party is the first thread in a destiny that he cannot escape, and trying to do so would be pointless.

His palms sweat as he balls his fists and tries to breathe slowly, calmly. Because really, he doesn't want to escape this fate. In the end, it promises peace. It promises freedom. It promises an end to his heart's eternal torment.

Ben thinks of my words again: 'A troubled road will lie ahead for you and she, which may lead to untimely death.'

Untimely death. He sighs. Much more preferable to a lifetime of heartache without Olivia. Much more preferable to a lifetime of love without love, something far more tragic than untimely death.

Looking up at the stars, Ben squints and tries to see his fate written there in brilliant and romantic splendour across the universe, which is all so much bigger than he. And far beyond his control. Because who is he to change any of it? He is no one. A mere mortal. A tiny sailboat bobbing about on the ocean of destiny.

'Well, fate, take a deep breath,' he whispers. 'And blow me along my course. Let's get this over with.'

And the cold, heavy thing in his chest, in his gut, pulses in rhythm, in excitement, and in terror, with every step that he takes as he finally enters the Rose's courtyard.

Strings of electric stars rise up into the heavens. A

white piano splendours on the decking, and a sweaty, grey-haired musician in a tux pounds out an old jazz tune. Laughter, murmured voices, and the clinking of wine glasses serve as the perfect percussion to his music.

Ben's heart pounds as he stops and stares around him, waiting for the gasp of recognition, and the hands on his shirt leading him right back out through those intricate gates. He throws a nervous look at Ross and Orlando, who gaze around calmly and don't look at all worried to be standing in enemy territory. Ben hopes that he is, like them, just as unrecognisable beneath the extra hair.

Leaning against a table covered in cheeses, olives, sun-dried tomatoes, crackers, and crystal glasses with skinny bellies full of sparkling white wine, Ben hesitates, then takes a flute and brings it to his lips. The sharp, sweet liquid of *Destiny* warms him from the inside out, and the ironic name of this new wine is not lost on him.

Christ. Ben grins as he places the empty glass back on the table. If his parents knew he was here, enjoying a glass of Rose Estate wine – Ouch! Maybe that's how his untimely death will come about. Murdered by his own incensed father.

Chuckling, he sucks a pimento from an olive, and scans the faces of the crowd, searching for those ocean-green eyes that he will never gaze into, those rosebud lips that he will never taste, that swan-like neck that he will never smell, that auburn hair in which he will never bury his face, those petal-perfect ears into which he will never whisper, I love you.

Ah, untimely death cannot come swift enough to end this torment.

Ben reaches for another glass of wine, but then he freezes.

He takes a step forward, then a step back as if the floor shifts beneath his feet and the world is now completely unbalanced.

She stands beside a table on the other side of the courtyard, nibbling on a cracker with bird-like beauty. She wears a long, white gown with bell sleeves. In contrast to the white material, her skin shines honey-gold and healthy and beautiful. Her smooth back is visible through crossed laces that weave all the way down, so low Ben can see she is not wearing underwear. Her eyes sparkle like two stones of onyx crystal. Her blonde hair is short, and kicks out in rebellious curls at the ends. Her tanned face is bright, and glows as if lit by an internal fire. So brilliant is her luminescence that Ben wonders if she originally taught fire itself how to burn, and flame itself how to crackle.

Then a man wearing a ridiculous T-shirt with a printed bowtie and cummerbund slithers into Ben's vision, and slides an arm around this woman's waist.

Oh, what Ben would give to be that man, to have his arm draped so casually around her. The man bends towards the beauty's ear, and just the thought of having his own lips that close to her skin makes Ben gasp in quick breaths.

She nods at whatever the man says, and Ben wishes she would look at him in that way, with those eyes, and that smile.

They place their empty glasses down, and walk hand in hand onto the patio, where couples sway to the slow song that the sweaty pianist now plays.

A pimply-faced waiter with an armful of empty trays and glasses rushes past and almost drops everything when Ben reaches out and grabs his sleeve.

'Excuse me,' Ben says, and points across the courtyard, 'do you know who that is?'

'I don't know, sir.' The waiter wrenches his arm away, and steadies his tray before hurrying off.

'But you didn't even look!' Ben calls out. 'Hey!'

Sighing in frustration, Ben turns back towards *her*, and is startled by just how gorgeous she actually is, and just a little bit frightened of the effect she has over him. He leans against the table, his legs weak.

She stands out from the rest of the women like a white diamond against the lobe of a dark-skinned ear. Like a dove amidst a flock of crows. And being pressed up against the dark skin of that guy just makes her glow all the brighter in contrast.

I have to meet her, Ben thinks. Speak to her, touch her hand, anything. Because, Jesus, have I ever *really* loved before now? My eyes have lied to me! Orlando was right:

all this time, I've been clouded with meagre crushes, for I swear I've never seen *true* beauty until tonight.

As he moves around the room, closer to her with each thrilling step, Ben knows he is closing in on his destiny. *She* is the reason he came here tonight. *She* will make him love like nothing else ever has. *She* will make him live like nothing else ever has.

Or ever will.

Because *she* is the one who will end his life.

chapter six

Claude spills his God damn wine all over his new God damn shoes when a careless God damn idiot bumps into his shoulder. He turns to scowl at whoever it was that just ruined his Italian leather, and the idiot mutters a vague apology, 'Oh, I'm so sorry, forgive me,' and then just moves away.

But Claude knows that voice.

He stares at the back of the man's head, but can't place him. His face is hidden beneath a bushy beard, which almost looks fake, and it's not until the man steps into a circle of light and turns his face at just the perfect angle.

He's an effing *Starre*! What the hell is he doing here?

Claude storms up to his father and stabs a shaking finger in Ben's direction. 'Look!' Claude snarls. 'There's a Starre here!'

Shepherd Rose turns from the man he'd been talking with and squints at the dark curls, and the blue eyes, and the bad synthetic beard that does nothing to disguise him now. 'Young *Ben*, isn't it?'

'That's him. The bastard.'

'Calm down, son,' Shepherd chuckles, placing a hand on Claude's shoulder.

Claude stares at his father. Calm down? What the hell?

'Leave the boy alone, he seems harmless enough. I've heard he's actually a ... a good kid.'

'What?' Claude gasps, not believing what he's hearing. How much has his father had to drink?

'Just ignore him.' Shepherd smiles. 'And stop frowning!'

'No!' Claude shakes his head. 'No, he's not welcome here. It'll ruin my whole night! He's already ruined my shoes! I won't put up with him here!'

The friendly smile on Shepherd's face morphs into a grimace. 'Yes, you will!' He takes a step forward, towering over Claude and whispering loudly, 'Am I the boss here, or are you? God, help me! You'll start a fight among my guests! You'll ruin my launch! There will be chaos! It will be *your* fault; *you'll* be the agitator! Not him!'

'But it's an insult having him here, drinking *our* family's wine!'

Shepherd flinches and Claude thinks he's finally gotten through to him.

But then Shepherd leans even closer. 'You listen to me, you little bastard!' He breaks away from Claude to flash a quick smile at a passing guest, then rounds on Claude again.

Claude wants to take a step away, but he stands his ground; the hell if he will show his father any sense of weakness.

'Get the hell away from me,' Shepherd hisses. 'I don't want to see you again for the rest of the night. And if you so much as say one word to that boy, you'll be *very* sorry!' And then he claps Claude on the shoulders and walks off, laughing loudly, and draping his arm around the creepy old guy he'd been talking to before.

Two women beside Claude glance away, laugh, and then put their heads together, whispering. About *him*, Claude would bet. They heard every word his father had just said. They saw him get treated like a God damn child!

His whole body shakes and his blood surges with adrenaline. He has to get out of here. Now.

In his haste, Claude knocks a pimply-faced waiter to the ground, but doesn't stop to help the kid up. In his room, he paces the floor and plots ways to make Ben Starre pay for this humiliation, to ensure that this night does not end without shedding at least one drop of that man's blood. Somehow, some way, thinks Claude, Ben Starre will pay for this.

chapter seven

Delia is being gazed at with such a gentle intensity that it makes her fingers tingle. Katherine is right: Guy Shylock is gorgeous. And he smells amazing. He is so close, she feels the throb of his heart, and the way it speeds up when her eyes lock on his. It's a very heady feeling knowing you have that effect over someone.

Delia turns away from him as soft applause and wolf-whistles thread through the room; her parents have stepped out on the dancefloor. They sway in perfect time with each other's bodies, and they stare at each other in the way they always do, and Delia knows that even though they are surrounded by a crowd, her parents are suddenly the only two people in the whole world.

As she watches them, she feels the usual bubbly warmth that carbonates through her blood – a mixture of pride and jealousy – and she thinks about the way they met.

Imogen had been on a date at her apartment, planning

on a quiet night in – a cheesy pizza and an equally cheesy movie. Until, that is, the pizza delivery guy had arrived. When she'd opened the door to take her food, Imogen looked up into those blue eyes of Shepherd Rose. They were a blue as immeasurable as the sea. A blue so striking, Imogen said she forgot all about her date squirming behind her on the sofa.

When she had handed Shepherd the money and their skin touched, they'd both been shocked by a surge of power that snapped between their fingertips.

Imogen always told Delia this was the force of their love, unable to be contained by their bodies. And her father would laugh and roll his eyes and say that it was just static electricity, dear. But then he would smile and look at his beloved wife, and Delia knew that he believed every single clichéd word that Imogen said.

So, that night, Imogen had invited Shepherd in, and they'd sat together on the couch, talking and eating the pizza, and all the while, the poor other guy – and to this day Imogen can't even recall his name – had sat there awkwardly, being ignored until at some point he'd eventually left, and neither Imogen nor Shepherd noticed him leaving.

Needless to say, Shepherd lost his job that night. But he says it was worth it. That although he lost his job, he found the greatest treasure in the world.

Delia has always loved this story. She loves the passion in her mother's voice every single time she tells it. She loves the tears of joy that fill her mother's eyes all these years later. And she loves that, even after so long, her parents still gaze at each other as if for the first time. As if they are falling in love all over again with every single glance.

Looking away from her parents swaying together on the dance floor, Delia gazes up at Guy. His eyes are open. They might be blue, but they are surely as deep as the sea. And his lips slowly, hesitantly, hungrily, move closer to hers. Although she is loving this headiness of knowing he wants her, she realises that it's not enough. She likes that he *likes* her. Perhaps she even loves that he *loves* her.

But Delia looks into Guy's eyes and there is no shockingly sudden spark.

Guy Shylock may be the sweetest man in the world. And she thinks he is very nice.

But she doesn't want *sweet*.

She doesn't want *nice*.

She wants ...

Delia looks over at her parents again.

She wants *that*.

Delia can hear Katherine rolling her eyes and telling her that love is not an instant thing, blah blah, and that she didn't give poor Guy enough of a chance, blah blah, and how could she possibly know that Guy wasn't *him* in such a short amount of time, blah blah.

Well fine, then.

Fine.

She *will* give him a chance.

Delia takes a long, calming breath, clearing her thoughts of everything else, and she lifts up on her toes to press her lips on his.

Guy freezes for a second. Holds his breath. Perhaps even his heart stops in shock.

She splays her hands across the breadth of his hard chest, and she feels his heart thump madly beneath her skin, and she feels the heat of his exhalation on her mouth, and Jesus, that is a wild thrill. She pulls back, breathes, and leans forward again. This time she parts her lips, and he copies her, and on her tongue she feels the vibrations of his sigh. Opening her eyes, she watches him kiss her. But his eyes are closed now and she can't see into the depths of him, and she can't see the way this kiss affects his very soul.

But over Guy's shoulder, she *can* see Katherine jumping up and down in jealous excitement. And she *can* see her father, beaming at her with what looks like relief.

Relief?

It hits her then. That if the prophecy is real, then Guy Shylock may be the only way she can change her destiny and save her life. If she gives him a chance, and if she falls in love with Guy, then she will not fall in love with anyone else, and she will not end up killing herself as a result of that romance.

And how hard can it really be to make yourself fall in love?

Surely, it can't be that hard. People fall in love every day. Why should she be any different?

She closes her eyes again, and tries to lose herself in this moment, with this man who is going to save her life. With this man who she knows wants her – even though she doesn't want him. Not yet, anyway. But she will. She *will* fall in love, because, if she doesn't she is going to die. Simple.

Maybe alcohol will help?

As she steps away from his kiss, she smiles. She loves that he takes a moment before opening his eyes, as if he doesn't want to ever return to the real world. She loves that when he finally does sigh and look down at her, that his eyes shimmer with happiness.

She feels something buzz inside her stomach. Hope, perhaps? Or maybe even the first minute stirrings of longing?

'I'm going to get us some drinks,' she says. 'Meet you back here?'

He nods. 'I won't move an inch. I'll be right here, wearing this.'

She laughs, and as she walks away, she turns and sees him watching her. He winks, and she feels the warmth in her stomach grow hot.

That's him, she tells herself. That's the man I'm going to fall in love with.

And suddenly, Delia feels her eyes prickle and her face grow hot and her throat close over. She runs through the crowd to the deserted back porch where nobody will see her tears of dissapointment fall.

As each salty drop splatters the porch railing, she thinks of everything she may be about to give up by forcing love with the violent hand of determination, rather than coaxing it with the gentle touch of innocence.

But in the end, love is love, right? It shouldn't really matter how it comes to be, as long as it arrives in the end.

And so what if there is no spark with Guy? There will be.

So what if there is no excitement? There will be.

So what if there is no instant knowing? She can live without that.

Because, at least, she will be *alive*.

She hears footsteps behind her and feels Guy's hand enclose her own. She gasps at his sudden touch. At the snap of static electricity that echoes through her. Her entire skin tingles from just having him close. And she almost lets out a sob of relief, because she knows that he really *is* the one, after all. Maybe it wasn't as instant as it had been with her parents, but it had come; it had just taken a little longer to reach her.

Closing her eyes, she loses herself in this moment, with this man who is going to save her life. With this man who she knows wants her – and who she suddenly wants too. With this man who she can feel herself suddenly, and instantly, falling in love with.

'I'm sorry if I cross the line by doing this,' he whispers,

and his words are muffled by the beautiful bliss that pounds in Delia's veins, 'but I just had to touch your angelic hand. And if I *have* crossed the line, if I have marred your skin with my own, then let me smooth away my unworthy touch with a gentle kiss.'

She feels his lips hot in the palm of her hand. Her heart races, her breath is trapped in her throat, her world spins, but inside this moment, with Guy's lips against the soft skin of her hand, time simply stops and Delia wishes they could live inside this eternity forever, and never return to the real world.

When he releases her, she curls her fingers around his warm kiss, holding it as tight as a secret.

And then, the real world screams itself back to reality with massive sensory overload.

The first thing Delia notices is that the timbre of Guy's heartbeat is different to before.

The second thing Delia notices is that Guy's smell is far more enticing. Do our senses change when the chemical of love is added?

The third thing Delia notices, as she opens her eyes and focuses on Guy's lovely face, is that the man she smiles up at is *not* Guy Shylock at all.

And the fourth thing: she does not care.

He stares at her, unblinking, with eyes as blue as and immeasurable as the sea.

'You said I'm angelic?' she says to this stranger. 'I'm no angel, but even if I was, I would never refuse the touch of a mere mortal such as yourself. Angels will gladly touch hands with even the lowest in society, if they're willing.' She lifts her hand, and when he smiles and presses his palm to hers, she feels the heat in her stomach bloom outward and she wonders how her thin, permeable layer of skin can possibly keep it contained inside her. 'Palm to palm is a form of sacred kiss.'

A crooked smile pulls at the corner of the stranger's mouth. 'Both angels and mortals have *lips*.'

Delia laughs softly. 'Lips they use to *pray* with.'

When he steps closer she stops breathing.

'Well, angel,' he whispers. 'Could we let lips do what hands do? Pray, and cleanse me of my sins.'

Oh, Jesus Christ, who the hell *is* this guy?

She gazes up at him in absolute pure awe, and she hears herself answer her own question with pride and simple certainty: *he is my one.*

He leans so close his energy seeps into her skin, but he does not kiss her.

He just hovers there, waiting. Waiting for her to fall.

But, Christ, she can't do this. She can't kiss him. Already, the absence of his touch is like a drug, and she wants more. She needs more. One kiss will be the end of her, because one kiss will never be enough.

Right now, she can still walk away. Right now, she can go back to Guy and live a long life with him. But right now, she doesn't even care if she dies. She doesn't care if she dies, just as long as she lives long enough to feel this man's lips on hers.

She lifts her chin.

She defies the stars.

And she seals her fate with a righteous kiss.

'So,' she whispers. Her hot breath bounces back from the closeness of his mouth, but she does not move away, not even an inch. 'Are my lips tainted with all your sins now?'

'By the sins from my lips?' He smiles.

And inside that smile, Delia sees her own death.

'We can't have that, can we?' he says. 'I'd better take my sins back again.'

When he kisses her for the second time, she feels as if she is cheating destiny. For isn't she supposed to put up some kind of fight? Isn't she supposed to want to live? Yet, as this handsome, bold stranger pulls her closer, she knows that she will gladly give her life, if that is the price she must pay. She will pay it without struggle. And she will not give destiny the fight it was surely expecting.

And maybe that is the only way she will defeat fate.

'What's your name, mortal?' Delia is not sure if she speaks out loud, not sure if her lips even *work* at their mundane job of producing words after having experienced such enlightenment through his kiss.

'Delia!'

She whirls around to see Katherine gaping. Her eyes

are so wide Delia can see the whites all the way around the pupils.

'Your mother is looking for you!' Katherine says. Her words are fast and clipped.

'I'll be right back.' Delia squeezes the hand that now holds her heart. She keeps the stranger in her vision for as long as possible, as Katherine drags her away.

Please, Delia sends out a silent plea to the gods, if you will only give us more time together, however short, then I swear I will not fight you. I will agree to go to my death willingly if you let me see him just one more time. Just one. And then I'll be satisfied.

In the doorway beside her parents, Delia nods and smiles to the departing guests, all the while looking over their heads to where she can see the stranger waiting near the corner of the house.

A group of people suddenly close around him, blocking him from her view. She sees flashes of him through the crowd as they usher him away towards the driveway.

'He's leaving!' Delia hisses to Katherine, her voice coming out fast and high-pitched. 'Why is he leaving?'

'Delia,' Katherine whispers, 'do you know who that is?'

Yes, Delia thinks, he is my one. But she shakes her head and says, 'No. Why? Do you? Who is he?'

Katherine grins. 'You didn't even ask him his name! You slut! I'm so proud!'

Delia grabs Katherine's hand and drags her to where they won't be overheard because she simply cannot hold the words inside her for one more second. 'He is fascinating! He kissed my hand! I mean, he actually kissed it, like in an old Laurence Olivier movie or something. Who does that these days? And the way he talks, God, no one has ever spoken to me like that before. You have to tell me now: who is he? You *do* know, don't you? Oh, God! What if he leaves, and I never see him again?'

'I don't think you need to worry about that,' says Katherine, prying Delia's fingers off her arm. 'He wants to see you again.'

'How do you know?'

She shrugs. 'I saw the way he was looking at you.'

'What do you mean? In what way was he looking?'

'Sort of like this.' Katherine's eyelids droop beneath raised eyebrows, her mouth falls slack, her tongue lolls from between smiling lips.

'You idiot!' Delia elbows Katherine and laughs. 'Where is he? Do you still see him?'

'Um ... yes, there! Standing by the gate with that group of people.'

Just as Delia finds his moon-bright face in the departing crowd, just as the relief floods her at seeing his smile once again, he slips through the gate and is gone from sight. She turns back to Katherine. 'Who is he? Do you know? Because if you don't, go and ask! Now!'

She pushes Katherine in the direction of the

driveway, but Katherine laughs and wriggles away. 'I know who he is,' she says, shaking her head, 'and I can't believe that you *don't*.'

'What? Tell me! Who is he?'

Katherine blinks, and then says the words Delia knew would be coming, 'Ben Starre.'

'Ben?' Delia whispers.

'The son of your great enemy.' Katherine pulls Delia closer and whispers fiercely, 'Your only love sprung from your only hate! Too early seen unknown, and known too late! Prodigious birth of love it is to thee, that you must love a loathed enemy.'

'Let me guess,' Delia says, her voice weakened, 'Shakespeare?'

'Spooky, huh? This is just like the play.'

'No, it's not,' she says, and her eyes fly wide as she grabs hold of a new kind of salvation. 'It's just a coincidence.'

'Coincidence?' Katherine laughs. 'Yeah, right. It's just a coincidence that your family and his family are lifelong enemies, like the Capulets and the Montagues.'

'Who?'

'And it's just a coincidence that you meet Ben at a party during which your parents are trying to set you up with Guy, the same way Juliet meets Romeo while being set up with Paris.'

'Who?'

'It's just a coincidence that ...'

'Okay, okay!' Delia looks back out to where the hungry darkness swallowed Ben whole. 'Why didn't I recognise him?'

'Well, as you said before, your parents weren't too enthusiastic about organising play dates together.' Katherine turns her eyes to the darkness as well, searching for him. 'Will you promise me one thing?'

'What?'

'Don't marry him! Romeo and Juliet got married the day after they met, and within three days they were both dead!'

Delia laughs nervously: too loud and too hysterical. 'Don't be ridiculous, Katherine! Why would I get married?'

'Just promise.' She stares at Delia, as if maybe she has seen the truth in her eyes, as if maybe she knows the agreement Delia just made to the gods of destiny, as if maybe she knows what is inevitably on its way.

'Okay,' Delia promises. 'I will not marry Ben Starre.'

And as her friend nods and smiles and relaxes, Delia wonders if maybe that simple detour from the Shakespearean plotline will be enough to save them all.

chapter eight

She's a *Rose?*

Oh, God damn it all.

Ben replays the words that were said to him by a waiter, hoping that if he hears them in his head enough times he'll realise she didn't actually say *Delia Rose*, but instead, some other collection of syllables.

Dee La Rose.

Deel Yarose.

Delia Rose.

Christ.

He finally finds love. *Real* love. Only to find it is a love born from his only hate.

Not that he *hates* the Roses. Not even Claude. But he's *supposed* to hate them, on principle.

'Let's go, bro!' Orlando grabs his arm.

'No.' Ben pulls free. 'I can't go yet.'

'Forget about Olivia, will you! You should *see* the girls I've lined up for us. Twins! One of them is a gymnast!'

Orlando grabs him again, and with a sigh, Ben is dragged away down the driveway. There is nothing else he can do here anyway. It's not as if he can just stroll up to Delia now, not with her parents right there, and Claude skulking somewhere in the shadows.

Like a handful of released marbles rolling in every direction, clunking into each other and bouncing away, the group of drunken men and women staggers down the driveway of the Rose household. Ben dawdles in a straight line behind them, feeling as if a giant rubber band has looped around his chest, and the other end remains looped around Delia's. Every step he takes away from her stretches the elastic tighter, makes it more difficult for him to put distance between them.

When he finally gets through the big wrought iron gates, which are closed and locked behind them with a clang, he stops, unable to take another step. The elastic has reached its limits and will give no more.

Panic swirls in him. He is trapped here. He is physically trapped here in this spot, unable to go back, unable to go forward. He is figuratively trapped here in this moment of choice. And as he hovers in the very same shadows that cloaked him earlier tonight, his mind draws me to him, and once again he hears my warning: '*An old desire will fade out and die; new love reincarnate in its place. Beauty, which was thought to be so bright, will pale compared to new desire's face. Unlike old love that once had seemed so true, new love will be returned with equal depth. A troubled road will lie ahead for you and she, which may lead to untimely death. Dripping fangs of guilt will pierce your soul, and vengeance-seeking venom infect your mind. One bite will drive you out – or drive you home. More strength to smile than to respond in kind. Love conquers all, a proverb that's on cue, for you may prove this old adage is true.'*

Well, Ben sighs, the first part of the prediction has come true. But, he wonders if it came true simply because it had been predicted to do so? Did Ben subconsciously seek out a new girl to fall for in order to act out his predicted destiny? If he had never visited me in the first place would he have attended this party tonight? Would he have seen Delia Rose? And would he now be torn between the fear of his impending death and the anticipation of bliss that its lead up will bring him?

Draping the invisible cloak of darkness tight around his shoulders, he steps backwards into the shadows and presses against the high sandstone wall that surrounds the property. His hands slide over the smooth stone, fingertips searching for any crack or crevice that may be deep enough to insert his toes, which are no longer weighed down, but instead light and floatingly buoyant.

The voices of Orlando and Ross get louder with proximity, and Ben holds his breath, crouches behind a tree and becomes a statue of the night.

'Because, he's *smart*,' says Ross. 'I bet he's gone home to bed.'

'Smart?' mutters Orlando. 'He's an idiot! I saw him

run back this way; he's gone after that bloody lesbian lorelei. Guess love makes you do stupid things.'

'Maybe that's because only the stupid fall in love.'

'You used to be in love with Ben,' Orlando huffs.

'Exactly!' Ross laughs and slaps himself on the forehead. 'I was *stupid!*'

'So ...' Orlando kicks at a pile of loose gravel with his toe. 'So, you don't want to fall in love again?'

Ross cocks his head to the side and gazes at Orlando with narrowed eyes and a sideways smile. 'What do you care, Mr New-Girl-Every-Night?'

'It's not that I *care* as such ... it's just that ... I mean, you know? Was just asking.' He coughs and spins away from Ross to face the wall again. 'Ben!'

'I'll get him to come out,' whispers Ross. Throwing his head back, and arms out wide, he yells: 'Oh, Ben! By the brightness of Olivia's eyes, I summon you! By her smooth forehead and red lips!' He mockingly runs his hands over his face and mouth as he calls out. 'By her fine foot,' he bends over and runs his fingers up from his toes, 'straight leg and,' digging his fingers into the flesh of his calves, he continues to move his hands higher up his legs, 'and quivering inner thigh!' Ross parts his legs and moves his hands over himself. 'Oh! By her sweet, warm juiciness, appear to us!'

'Stop it!' Orlando croaks and drags a hand down his face. 'Dear *God*. That is so not appealing.'

'What?' Ross grins. 'My words were fair and honest;

I'm only using the name of the woman he loves – and the parts of her he will *never have* – to lure him out.'

'Yeah, being reminded of something you *can't* have!' Orlando mutters. 'That'll work.'

'What?'

'What? No, nothing, I didn't say anything.'

Ross shrugs and turns back to face the wall. 'Okay, Ben!' he yells. 'Goodnight, then! Orlando and I are going home to bed!' He glances over at Orlando and laughs. 'Not together, obviously!'

'Yeah, no, of course not,' Orlando laughs, too, but it's a quick, high laugh.

'You think we should?' asks Ross.

Orlando whirls around and blinks at Ross. His eyes are wide and his face is suddenly as bright as the moon. 'Do *you?*'

'I meant,' says Ross, narrowing his eyes, 'should we *leave?*'

'Oh! Yeah, no, I knew what you meant.' Orlando looks away and coughs again. 'It's no use looking for Ben if he doesn't want to be found.'

Turning, Ross stumbles back to the weaving gaggle of drunkards, where a waiting man rests a hand comfortably in the back pocket of Ross's jeans. Orlando hesitates before sandwiching himself between two elfish brunettes in dresses so short they shouldn't have even bothered putting them on.

How can those two, Ben wonders as he stands and

stretches his cramping thighs, make fun of such a thing as unrequited love? And they say that *I'm* the stupid one.

Looking up at the tree he is crouched behind, he sees its branches reach almost to the top of the wall. Without pausing to let any type of rational thought poison his mind, Ben climbs, pressing against it like a lover, and then drops down amongst the labyrinthine lines of the Rose Estate vineyard.

Rows and rows of tall, wide grapevines stretch to the edge of his vision. Each row is draped in white bird netting like a virginal bride's veil, and as he reaches out a hand towards it, a torch beam blinds him.

He drops to the ground.

The light follows.

He crouches amid the grapes.

The light holds him still.

He wraps himself in the camouflage of the netting.

The light strokes his naked face like an uninvited seducer.

If he is found trespassing on Rose property, he will be in serious trouble. Christ, Sergeant Burgundy is just itching for a scapegoat.

He huddles even smaller, praying his bass drum heart is not as loud as it is in his ears.

And then it is dark.

Floating blue blobs dance in his vision, but soon his molested eyes adjust to the friendly darkness.

Only to be once again blinded.

Because it is not a security guard waving his torch about and posing a threat of arrest. Instead, it is the one who poses even more danger to him than anyone or anything else.

Right before his eyes, Delia passes, shining like the sun in the east. Shining so brightly that her glow eclipses that of the envious moon above, who must be sick and pale with jealousy.

She walks with her back to him, along a row of vines, her fingers trailing the bird netting while her torch beam dances ahead.

On his hands and knees, Ben creeps along the next row of grapes, in step with Delia's feet and her moving light; the very need to be close to her pulls his heart alongside like a magnet.

She stops walking and gazes up, her eyes lost in the beauty of the sky. Beside her, unseen, Ben gazes up, too, lost in the beauty of her face. God, he cannot physically look away. It's as if the two most beautiful stars in heaven have swapped places with her eyes. They shine. They twinkle from inside her two delicate sockets, while her real eyes glimmer above them in the sky, throwing out so much luminescence that he wouldn't be surprised if birds start singing, thinking it's morning already.

And then she sits.

Right there on the dirt.

Right there beside him.

With only a grapevine separating them.

He watches her through breaks in the leaves. Her legs are crossed, one elbow rests on a knee, and her cheek rests against her palm.

And he's never been more jealous of anything as he is right then, of her own God damned hand!

'Oh, wow.' Delia lets out a long, sorrowful sigh. 'I just can't believe it.'

Ben's body clenches like a fist at the pleasurable shock of hearing her speak.

'I just can't believe that it's *Ben,*' she says.

And at the sound of *his* name coming from *those* lips, his body clenches up even tighter.

Had she seen him drop down over the wall?

Does she know he is hiding here?

And who is she talking to? Perhaps she isn't alone after all.

'Ben.'

She speaks his name again and he wants to cry from the exquisite pain of it. But he holds himself still and silent.

'Why does it have to be *Ben?*' she says. 'What if he changed his name, and wasn't a Starre anymore? Would that make a difference? Or, if I knew that he truly wanted me,' she shrugs, 'I could no longer be a Rose.'

What? Ben's mind spins. Did she mean that? Could she really mean that? Jesus!

Even if he wants to speak now, he can't; he has been forced mute by shock.

Besides, she still could be speaking to someone else. She remains cross-legged, staring upwards, as if in conversation with only the stars above. But what if he speaks, what if he reveals himself only to discover that there *is* someone there, someone hidden to him just like he is hidden to her? Then he'll be dragged away, arrested for trespassing, or maybe even stalking. Burgundy will gladly lock him away for breaking the new intervention order to show the town that he is serious about ending this feud. And Ben's entire fate will be altered.

What if he is locked away for days, or weeks, or months? Could he handle such a long stretch of time without seeing this new sunshine? Could he handle spending *any* amount of time in a dark-filled world after witnessing the addictive beauty of such light? And what about the prophecy? Is there a time limit on the fulfilment of destiny? If it gets delayed, does that mean it resets, and Delia will never be his salvation but his unravelling through heartache and vitamin D starvation?

'If you think about it, it's only his surname that's the problem,' continues Delia, still staring up at the sky. 'He is *Ben*; he's not *Starre*. What is Starre, anyway? It's not as if it's a *part* of him; it's not a hand, nor foot, nor arm, nor face, nor any other part of his body. Oh, why can't he have some other surname? What's in a name, anyway? I mean, if we used a different word for *flower* it would still smell just as sweet.' She grins then. 'Like, if a *rose* was called a *star*, perhaps? Ben would still be just as perfect, whether his last name is Starre or not.'

Warm coppery blood seeps onto Ben's tongue as he bites down on his lip.

And as Delia shuffles on the spot, Ben sees exactly to whom she is talking.

His muscles bunch in readiness to move.

'I wish he would get rid of his name,' she says, 'in exchange for me!'

'Deal!' Ben jumps to his feet and almost shouts. 'Just say the word, and I will no longer be known as "Ben Starre".'

As she gasps and scrambles backwards, she drops her phone. The screen, glowing as the voice recorder ticks through the seconds of a verbal journal entry, falls face down in the dirt.

Liquid night surges forward to drown them both.

Ben hears her fingers searching across the ground. When she grasps her phone, Delia raises it up to shine light on Ben's face.

'Ben?'

'Yes,' he answers. 'Although I'll happily change my name if you want me to.'

Her voice drops low and her head whips about searching for anyone who might have seen him. 'How did you get over the walls?'

'No walls can keep love out!'

'If you are found in here, you'll be arrested! Unless

Claude finds you first. If he sees you here, he'll kill you! I don't know what you did to him tonight, but he's really pissed.'

'One loving look from you and I'll be forever pardoned of any crime I could ever commit; there'll be nothing your family, or Burgundy, could do to me,' he says. 'But, if you *don't* love me, well then that's as good as death anyway; I may as well march right up to Claude's room myself.'

'How did you know where I was?' she asks, still looking around.

'I didn't.' Ben pauses and waits for her to stop, to look at him, to see into his soul. 'Fate brought me to you.'

She hesitates at this, then finally turns her face away. 'I can't believe you were sitting there the whole time.' She groans, burying her face in her hands. 'Did you hear everything I was saying?'

Leaning over the vines, Ben reaches for her hands and frees her face. 'From the very second I saw you tonight, it's like, I don't know, something came alive inside me!'

Suddenly she rips her hands from him and steps backwards. 'No, you're just saying that!'

'I'm not, I swear,' Ben says.

She rolls her eyes. 'Just saying "I swear" doesn't prove you're telling the truth.'

'Delia Rose, I swear by the moon above–'

'Oh, don't swear by the moon!' she cries, rushing forward again to thankfully take his hand, which had grown chilled with the absence of her touch. 'The moon is constantly changing, and if you swear by that, then who's to say that your feelings won't change, too?'

Ben laughs then, feeling almost high at all of this: her touch, her words, her panic. 'Well, what should I swear by? God?'

'Yes,' she says. 'But don't swear on *the* God, swear on *my* God. So swear on *yourself.*'

His cheeks burn at these words.

She thinks he's a *god*?

'Wait, no, this is too impulsive.' She drops his hands again. 'I don't know how many glasses of wine *you* had tonight, but I don't want it to be like this: professing our drunken love while hiding in between rows of grapes! You might wake up tomorrow with a hangover and regret every word you are saying right now.' She is shaking her head and backs away, fast, along the vines.

'No, wait!' Ben calls, tripping over his words as he hurries along beside her. 'You can't leave without satisfying me!'

'*Excuse* me!' She stops then, and crosses her arms. 'What sort of *satisfaction* are you expecting?'

'Not *that*,' he says quickly. 'I'm not like that. I just mean, well, I told *you* I love you. But you didn't tell me how you feel.'

'What?' Her eyes widen. 'I said that before I even knew you were listening!' With her hands on her hips, she narrows her eyes. 'Although, I wish I could take it back now.'

And just like that, Ben's smile falls from his lips and shatters at his feet. 'Why?'

'So I can say it to you, for the first time, all over again!' She rushes forward, leaning as far as she can over the tall vines, to press her lips to Ben's.

She is a breath away from him when a voice rings through the still night air like a tolling bell.

'Did you hear that?' Delia's dark, glittering eyes blaze wide. 'Someone's calling me! I have to go inside. Can I see you tomorrow?'

Ben shakes his head. 'No, I don't want to do that.'

There's a beat of silence. 'You don't want to see me?'

'I don't want to *sneak around*. I don't want to hide our relationship as if it is wrong or dirty. We are adults after all!'

'Relationship?' She smiles. 'Wow. So what are we supposed to do? We can't just meet up in the middle of the town square! Could you imagine what people would say? And this new intervention order that Burgundy has drawn up actually *prevents* us from being within one hundred metres of each other. You know that, right? Your father had to sign it, too.'

'I don't care about any of that,' Ben says. 'I just want to be with you, openly, proudly, easily.'

'Well then, Mr Starre, what do you propose we do?'

He grins at her. Because that was it. That was exactly the answer. She had said it herself already.

But surely, Ben thinks, there's no way she will agree to do *that*. It's totally crazy. But then this whole night had been totally crazy, right?

He takes her hand, and with difficulty, kneels down on one knee, barely able to still see her face over the grapevine between them. 'Delia Rose, will you turn a rose into a star and marry me?'

She pulls free and backs away as if he has burned her.

Damn. Too fast. Too crazy. But he keeps talking anyway, because really, this is the only way. 'Hear me out, okay? Meet me at Robin Goodfellow's house. He's a friend of mine. And a justice of the peace; he can marry us right away, and then we'll be legal. You'll be a Starre. There'll be nothing either of our families can do about it!'

She hesitates, chewing on her lower lip for so long Ben worries that soon the sun will rise and he'll get dragged away before he gets an answer.

Reaching for him, she touches the edges of the fake beard, and peels it slowly from his skin. Second by second, he is revealed to her, and as the cool night air caresses his face he exults in the freedom of this moment.

And then finally, *finally*, she speaks. Her voice is raspy, as if her thoughts have stripped it bare of all rationale. 'I'll meet you there. And if you stay true to your word, if you haven't changed your mind, then we'll be married, and I will follow you to the ends of the earth.'

Ben doesn't know how to physically hold this knowledge inside his body. The joy of it is so forceful he can feel it pressing on the inside of his skin, desperate to break free and soar.

'But,' Delia holds up a hand, 'if you do wake up and realise this was all a drunken mistake, or if it's all just a ploy to get into my pants tomorrow night, I ask you to please leave me alone now.'

'I won't change my mind,' he whispers. 'My soul depends on it.'

Her eyes glitter with what might be excitement, or what might be absolute fear, as she nods, gives a nervous laugh and says, 'I'll see you at the altar, then. Goodnight!' And then, she turns and runs.

Watching the soles of Delia's feet carry her away until the only thing left is the darkness and the memory of her words, Ben slumps forward, exhausted. His head droops, and his feet drag like anchors as he walks. He draws in a deep breath, a shaky breath, a breath so suddenly wet with fear that it's like breathing water.

What if this is all just a dream? Because, surely, this is all just too perfect, too wonderful, to be a part of conscious reality.

But it isn't a dream, it is my destiny, he thinks, as he forces himself to move through the sudden heaviness that fills him.

Walking away from Delia, from love, from the wonder

of this moment, reminds him of having to trudge his way through the school corridors towards a class he despises.

'Ben!' Her voice rings as clear as a bell and she is there, on the other side of the vines again, even more beautiful than Ben's memory paints her.

He races back, his inner schoolboy now rejoicing as if the final bell has rung to signal his freedom.

'What time tomorrow?' she asks.

'Nine o'clock.'

She sighs. 'It seems like twenty years until then.'

There is silence as they look at each other.

And then she grins. 'I forgot what else I was going to say.'

'That's okay,' he shrugs, 'I'll just stand here until you remember.'

'You'll have to stand there forever, because all I can think of now is you,' she says.

'Fine with me,' he says. 'I will definitely keep standing here, so that you keep forgetting!'

She shakes her head. 'No, I have to go; after all, I'm getting married in the morning!' She says it so simply. So easily. As if it's something she's been planning all along. 'Goodnight.' She backs away. 'Goodnight. I wish we could keep saying goodnight until tomorrow morning, when we'll be seeing each other again anyway.'

Watching Delia fold once again into the jealous embrace of night, Ben closes his eyes and counts off the minutes that remain in this day. For soon, it will be tomorrow.

Tomorrow.

And Ben wonders just how many tomorrows they both have left.

chapter nine

The grey-eyed morning smiles on the frowning night. It checkers the eastern clouds with streaks of light. Like a drunken man, the darkness stumbles out of the sun's path and tumbles down over the horizon, where it collapses to wait for the festive night to arrive again.

And before the sun rises high enough to burn away the morning dew, Puck gathers his ungroomed hair into a messy ponytail and slips out into the garden with his yoga mat.

Ah, Sunday, he thinks. Fabulous Sunday. The one day of the week where he doesn't have to conform to the dress code of the Establishment. Where he can be *Puck* instead of *Robin Goodfellow*, JP, responsible member of society. On Sundays he can wear his pink sandals, a dirty pair of ripped jeans, and a tie-dyed shirt. On Sundays he can be unshaven, and ungroomed, and uncaring. On Sunday's he can write poetry, and meditate, and get nice and good and stoned. Hell, yes.

He sits in the lotus position and brings his palms together in the Namaste pose and takes a breath, clearing his heart chakra, before touching his thumbs and forefingers together in a Gyan Mudra and turning his thoughts inward.

'Om.'

Okay, and breathe in. And keep the mind empty. And breathe out. Mind empty. Mind empty. Breathe in. Mind is still empty. Empty as a woven basket. The basket filling up with thoughts. Filling with poisoned weeds, and perfumed flowers, that each bloom equally in the garden of my consciousness. I will study them. Both the good thoughts and the bad thoughts. I will study them, and the medicinal properties that each one brings, as if they are nothing but plants pulled from the earth. For the earth is nature's mother, but also nature's tomb: after death, we return again to nature's womb.

Oh, that's deep, he thinks. Got to remember that one, yep. Should I stop and write that down? No. Focus, Puck. Breathe in.

'Om.'

The earth is nature's mother, but also nature's tomb. Plants and animals are born from our earth, and she provides these children with nourishment. Everything that nature gives birth to is born for a reason, or has some special quality, and each quality is different. Herbs, plants, and stones possess great healing power. Even the bad stuff.

'Om.'

There is nothing so evil that it does not provide the earth with some special good. Likewise, there is nothing so good that, if treated badly or in the wrong way, will not turn bad. Virtue, therefore, will turn to vice if it's misused. And vice to virtue through dignified muse.

Oh, this is good stuff, I need to write this all down.

Virtue will turn to vice if misused, and vice to virtue through dignified muse.

'Om.'

The clinking of the back gate, and the shush of grass beneath hurrying feet, pulls Puck's thoughts out by their roots, and he sighs and breathes out, and opens his eyes.

Ben Starre practically skips along the garden path. 'Puck!' he calls out, and grins and waves.

'What's happening, Benny? You look like doodie! I'm guessing you didn't get a wink of sleep again last night? Let me guess: Olivia?' Uncurling his pretzelled legs, Puck stands in one fluid movement, and looks Ben in the eye. 'You gotta get over this chick, man, she's killing you.'

Ben says nothing, just grins goofily.

'Wait ... what's that look for? Wide smile, light in your eyes that brightens your whole face. I'm guessing you haven't been to bed at all.' And Puck shakes his head, because he knows exactly what has caused his friend's smile. 'Well, not to *sleep* anyway.'

'Bingo.' Ben grins wider.

'With Olivia? But I thought she was ...' Puck's wavers a hand in the air. 'Not interested.'

'Olivia?' Ben laughs. He throws his head back and barks out a laugh so deep and genuine it brings actual tears to his bleary eyes. 'Olivia doesn't even *exist* for me anymore.'

'Finally!' Puck says. 'So if it wasn't Olivia who put that goofy grin on your face, then who?'

'I went to the Rose Estate wine launch last night, where I met and fell in love with Delia Rose.'

'What?' Puck frowns. Yes, okay, he saw Ben's lips form the shapes of that name, Delia Rose, but that just can*not* be what he'd said.

Ben shrugs. 'We're in love.'

'*You* and *Delia Rose* are in *love*?'

Ben's impossibly wide grin gets even wider, and Puck's head starts to spin.

'Man, I am far too straight for this conversation.' He turns and walks inside, calling over his shoulder. 'How the hell?'

'I'll tell you later; for now, though, I need a favour.' Ben's footsteps shadow Puck's through the back door. 'Can you marry us?'

'What?' Puck stops so quickly that Ben crashes into his back. 'When?'

'She'll be here at nine.'

'*This morning*? Holy hell, you've certainly changed your tune! How can Olivia, who you loved so much yesterday, be so quickly pushed aside today? Does love truly come from your heart, or from your,' Puck gestures to Ben's pants, 'eyes! Far out, man! How long have I listened to you cry over that girl? And now she's not even worth *thinking* of?'

'What do you care?' Ben frowns and crosses his arms. 'You hassled me continuously about loving Olivia.'

'For *obsessing*,' Puck corrects. 'Not *loving*. If you really loved her, you wouldn't be able to wave it away so easily.'

'You told me to get over her.'

'Yes, but I didn't expect you to do it so quickly!'

'Please, don't lecture me, man. Delia loves me back, okay. Olivia didn't.'

'So what? You think because one girl loves you back, where the other didn't, it indicates true love and a need for marriage?'

'This is different. This is deeper than anything I've ever felt.'

Sighing, Puck closes his eyes, trying to get centred.

Focus. Breathe in.

A Rose and Starre marriage? Ah, hell.

Or, maybe not?

Maybe not *hell* at all.

Maybe, in fact, it will bring about peace.

Peace!

Virtue will turn to vice if misused, and vice to virtue through dignified muse.

And he could, in fact, be that dignified muse. A

Justice of the Peace, actually creating peace. He has the power and the opportunity to transform a longstanding vice into a virtue. A Rose and Starre marriage.

Puck opens his eyes. 'I'll do it.'

'Really?' Ben grins. 'You'll perform the wedding?'

In answer, Puck holds up two fingers in a V. 'Make love, not war, brother. Let's go change the world.'

chapter ten

'So. Are you completely insane?' Katherine blows into Delia's kitchen like a storm, and holds up a hand, silencing Delia when she opens her mouth to answer. 'Wait. That was rhetorical, and I can't have this conversation yet; I need coffee. A strong one! Stat.'

Delia leans against the counter looking all beautiful and glowy and perfect, even at stupid-o-clock in the morning. 'Did you drive over here in your pyjamas?' she asks.

'What choice did I have?' says Katherine. 'You call me at the effing break of dawn to tell me that you and Ben effing Starre are effing eloping today, and I need to get here now because I'm your witness and your bridesmaid and you can't do it without me – which made me wonder if you actually know how a wedding works, because I think the groom is the one you can't do it without!'

'Keep your voice down,' Delia hisses and her eyes flick

up towards the ceiling. 'And anyway, I would have waited until you threw on some jeans.'

Katherine flaps her hands in the direction of the coffee machine until Delia finally floats over to it, looking so light and free she might have sprouted wings overnight. Maybe she really *is* in love, thinks Katherine. Bitch.

Filling two mugs, Delia places them on the bench and sits on the stool opposite Katherine, who blows the steam from her cup, and slurps at the coffee, and oh, thank God for caffeine! 'Okay.' She nods. 'Go.'

Delia takes a breath and then words just start tumbling from her lips. 'Well, after you left last night, I went for a walk in the vineyard, you know, recording my journal entry, and then he practically jumps out at me from the shadows, where he'd been hiding, listening the whole time. I was so embarrassed!'

Katherine's skin starts to tingle as she pictures what she is hearing, and then the image of Delia and Ben in the vineyard splices together with one of Romeo and Juliet on an effing balcony. 'Jesus, act two has started,' she mumbles into her coffee.

'Something magical happened last night,' says Delia. 'There was an instant connection, and he felt it too, I know he did!'

'Of course he did,' Katherine says. 'That's how it happens. It needs to be instant; Shakespeare only had two hours; there wasn't time for a long, drawn-out courtship on the stage.'

'Oh, come on, Katherine, will you drop it? I am not Juliet, and Ben is not Romeo. This is not a tragedy!'

'So why are you getting married after knowing each other for less than a day then? No one does that in real life.'

'Because, we can't be together any other way. The intervention order prohibits Roses and Starres from being in the same vicinity as each other. You know that. If we get married, I'll be a *Starre*. The legalities of the order won't apply to us anymore.'

'But ...' says Katherine, 'but ...' She stops speaking and just shakes her head, because actually, what Delia is telling her does kind of make perfect sense. Holy crap. 'But you do understand this is *insane*, right?'

'I know.' Delia laughs. 'I can hardly believe it!'

'And what about Guy?'

'Guy?' She frowns. 'What about him?'

'You promised to give him a chance, remember?'

'I did! I danced with him, but there was nothing there. No chemistry. No spark. Not like there is with Ben. So, now *you* can have Guy.'

'Oh, gee, thanks for your leftovers.' Katherine rolls her eyes, but then grins and shrugs. 'Oh, what do I care: I'll take it.'

Delia's laugh trills across the benchtops like the reverberation of a bell.

'Are you sure it's love, though?' Katherine asks. 'I mean, Ben is easily one of the hottest guys in town. It's probably just lust. Hell, by that definition, I've been in *love* with Ben Starre for years!'

'Katherine. I am in love with Ben,' Delia says. 'I *love* him!'

And Katherine sits back, stunned, because in that moment she knows that Delia is telling the truth. In that moment she has never been more jealous of her best friend. And in that moment, she has never been more terrified for her.

'You don't think you're moving just a little fast?' she asks. 'What if you marry him, and he turns you into someone you hate? What if you get to know him, only to find that you hate his guts?'

'Because we are meant to be together, and people who are meant to be together don't end up hating each other. Look at my parents.'

'Look at *my* parents,' Katherine mutters. 'Okay, well, what about the fortune teller's prediction?'

'What about it? She said I would fall in love, and I have.'

'Exactly! That part came true. What if the rest of it comes true as well?'

'Love conquers all? What's so bad about that? I hope it *does* come true!'

'That's not what I meant and you know it. What was

the line again? *Hatred buried by love's self sacrifice*, or something.'

Delia looks away. 'It won't happen.'

'But what if it does?'

'It won't!'

'How do you know?'

When she turns to face Katherine again, Delia's eyes blaze. 'Because love will conquer all.'

'I can't talk you out of this, can I?'

'Can't you just be happy for me?' Delia says.

Happy for her? How could she be *happy* about watching the person she loved most in this world drawing closer and closer to her own final act? How could she be happy about watching it all unfold before her eyes?

But then, Katherine blinks and sighs and smiles. 'Fine. Even if this prophecy thing *is* real, I know this play backwards. Don't worry, I'll rewrite your ending, even if it kills me. Which, of course it won't, because I'm probably one of the insignificant characters, like the nurse or something, and the nurse doesn't die at the end.'

chapter eleven

Ben chews his cheek and taps his legs and checks the clock every minute. Yeah, so he is nervous, but the hell if he will admit that.

'I hope this doesn't come back to bite us on the arse, my friend,' Puck says.

'Even if it does,' Ben shrugs, 'any excrement that may later hit the proverbial fan will be totally worthwhile. And anyway, once she is mine and I am hers, then nothing will be able to darken us. Not even death will stop our love. I wouldn't care if I died tomorrow, as long as I could have called her mine today.'

Puck smiles. 'That's beautiful, man. Hey, listen, can I give you a few words of wisdom dude, while we're waiting?'

'Shoot.'

'Well, you obviously feel quite passionate about this chick; any idiot can see that. Just be careful you don't overdo it; nurture that flame or you might burn yourselves out, you know? Run out of fuel. I've seen it happen too many times, bro. You know how many divorce papers I've signed just in the last six months?' He shakes his head. 'The secret to a long marriage is to take it slow and moderate, otherwise it may end in tragedy. Violent delights have violent ends.'

Ben nods once. 'Noted.'

And then the front door at the end of the hall opens and sunlight steps through. Following on the beautiful heels of this metaphoric bridesmaid, walks Delia Rose. Framed in the doorway, the light from outside haloes itself around her silhouette, and she shines.

Delia floats across the room, so weightless she could have walked on the thread of a spider's web without it snapping under her feet. Her short hair ends in curls that kick out all over her head, around which is draped a crown of crimson wildflowers. She wears a satin dress of deep burgundy, with tiny embroidered roses weaving themselves around her low neckline, sleeves, and the hem of her dress. Clasped in her slender fingers is a single red rose.

Behind her, wearing pink satin pyjamas and bunny slippers, walks the friend Ben saw the previous night.

'Hi,' Delia says, once she stops in front of Ben.

He nods.

'You still want to do this?' she asks.

He nods.

'You sure?'

He nods.

'You have to speak at least two words this morning,' she says. You know that, right?'

'I'm just so happy,' he says. 'I can't ... I just ... I have no words.'

'Maybe that's a good thing,' says Delia. 'Anyone who could sum up this feeling with adequate words would not be experiencing its true force.'

'If I may intercede.' Puck clears his throat. 'Let's get you two crazies hitched!'

Delia passes her rose to Katherine, and then takes Ben's hand. She simply steps forward and touches her skin to his skin, her palms to his palms, her fingers to his fingers, as if it is the most natural thing in the world. And maybe, Ben thinks, it *is*.

Together they step through into Puck's lounge, stand in the middle of the shag rug, and repeat the words instructed by Puck: 'The only thing I want; I have. My happiness is as immeasurable as the sea, my love as deep. The more I give to you, the more I have, for both are infinite.'

Then Puck smiles, and turns to Delia. 'Cordelia Rose, Benedick Starre, do you each take the other as your forever partner?'

'We do,' they say.

'Rings?' Puck asks.

Ben reaches into his pocket and withdraws a gold ring studded with flecks of ruby. 'This was my grandmother's.'

Turning to Katherine, Delia takes a white gold band with diamonds, which she slips onto Ben's finger, and says: 'My grandfather's.'

Puck beams. 'The choice of these two rings could not be more symbolically perfect: the final coming together of two families. May these rings bring you happiness and peace. Now, please face each other again, and hold hands. Allow me to incorporate two in one, and pronounce you husband and wife. You may ...'

But Ben is already kissing his wife, rushing headlong into a fate he dares to challenge, and all around them destiny smiles.

chapter twelve

Every oily chip that Orlando eats squirms in his stomach like a live worm; he feels it trying to wriggle back up again. Flashes of the previous night assault him, making him cringe and groan. He sees Ross leaving with that tall, blond idiot, in a tangle of arms and legs and lips, while Orlando had been left in the company of the beautiful and completely willing Dromio twins – a position in which any man in town would have killed to have been. Any other man, that is, but Orlando Starre. Well, and Ross Aylind, obviously. Oh, and the tall, blond idiot.

Orlando inhales another disgusting chip as again he sees himself falling through his front door, landing beneath the twins, and then rolling out from under them so fast they might have been on fire. He'd apologised, crawled to the phone, and called them a taxi, while they'd frowned in confusion and kissed him goodbye before he'd closed the door in their gorgeous faces.

Will they tell anyone that *the* Orlando Starre didn't

want them? That perhaps *the* Orlando Starre doesn't really like girls?

The chips in Orlando's gut roll violently as a shiny black convertible screeches to a stop at the curb, and Ross leaps out.

'Where the hell is Ben?' Ross says.

Ben, Orlando sighs. It's always about Ben.

Ross perches beside Orlando on the bench and the smell of floral aftershave rises up around them.

Orlando breathes it in.

'Did he go home last night?' asks Ross.

Orlando shakes his head, and the earth spins again. 'I just dropped into his place. His bed wasn't even slept in.'

'I bet it's that hard-hearted, carpet-muncher, Olivia,' Ross mutters. 'She's going to drive him to the loony ward.'

'There was a note taped to his front door, though. From Claude Rose.'

Ross rolls his eyes. 'One of his stupid challenges?'

Orlando nods. 'And you know Ben will answer it, too.'

'Anyone that can write can answer a note.' Ross smirks and grabs a handful of chips.

'I meant: he'll answer the challenge. Not the letter.' Orlando's head throbs, but he doesn't know if it's from the hangover or the heat pouring off Ross's skin.

'Doesn't matter anyway,' Ross shrugs. 'We've already lost him to love's fatal arrow. Do you think he has it together enough at the moment to win in a battle of wits? Especially against Claude Rose?'

'What's so good about Claude?' Orlando asks.

'As much as I hate to admit it,' says Ross, 'he *can* drive. It's like he sees everything in slow motion: time, distance, proportion. Not to mention that car of his.' He whistles and sighs.

Orlando thinks about his own ride, and how close he came to that cliff edge.

He wonders if Ross heard about that. But then, of course he would have; everybody heard about that.

'Let's get out of here,' Orlando says. 'It's hot and I'm not feeling too well. Besides, I don't want to bump into the Roses right now; the weather is hot enough without their egos boiling my blood.'

He crawls into Ross's car and lies across the backseat.

'You know who you remind me of?' says Ross, walking around to the driver's side. 'You're like one of those guys who goes to a bar and slaps his keys down on the table, saying: "I won't be needing these." But after the second drink he snatches them back, slurring that he is all right to drive.'

'What's that supposed to mean?' Orlando mutters.

'It means, you're all talk, Orlando Starre. You'll jump at any excuse to put your foot down. Take yesterday for example.'

Oh no, he cringes, here it comes.

'You were trying to stop that race between the

workers, right? But as soon as Claude insulted you, you were the one flying down the road. Lucky for you, I guess, that Mummy and Daddy turned up when they did.'

'What? You don't think I could've beaten him?'

'No offence, honey, but no.'

'I suppose you think *you* could have?' Orlando huffs.

'I'd come closer than you would, any day.' Ross winks and all Orlando's frustration and embarrassment and nausea washes away.

'Anyway,' says Orlando, 'what are you even doing here? Why aren't you home with your new *friend* from last night?'

'What does *he* have to do with racing against Claude Rose? And what do you care who I go home with?'

'Just forget it.'

Ross crosses his arms. 'No, tell me, Orlando. What's with this jealous boyfriend act all of a sudden?'

'I'm not jealous!'

'You didn't seem to care about me last night when you went home with the Bimbo Twins!'

'As a matter of fact, I did care!' Orlando yells. The words echo through his throbbing skull and he sees something brighten in Ross's face.

Oh, hell. Why did he say that? Here comes the realisation, and then the laughter, and then the rejection.

And soon the whole town will know.

And soon his father ...

'You always *what*?' Ross asks.

'Nothing. Can we drop it, please?' Orlando turns his eyes away.

'No, we can't. You always *what?*'

'Ross!' Orlando pleads.

'Orlando!' he copies the whiney tone. 'Come on, tell me!'

'Tell you what?'

'Tell me you like me!' Ross yells.

'Well, yeah, maybe I do!' Orlando yells back.

'Yeah? Well, maybe I like you, too!'

'Yeah?' Orlando shouts. 'Fine!'

'Fine!'

'So, what are we going to do about it?'

'We could stop yelling at each other!' Ross's face relaxes into a laugh.

Nausea pools once again in Orlando's gut; a frothing swirl of nerves and relief and red-hot desire. 'So, what now?'

'We could go back to my place?' says Ross.

And just like that, Orlando's lips curl into an easy smile. He feels his true self stepping forward for the first time in his life. 'Ross Alind, what type of boy do you think I am?'

'My type,' says Ross. He leans between the front seats and kisses Orlando full on the mouth, and everything is suddenly right in the world.

'You should know,' Ross whispers, 'I'm not the

patient type.' His words taste hot. 'How about we just park somewhere and put the top up?'

And then Ross is in the back seat. And then his hands are on Orlando's skin. And then the whole world is shining bright as chrome. And Orlando radiates in this new light.

'Sorry to interrupt, but may I have a word with one of you?'

And then the whole world stops turning.

Orlando freezes beneath Ross's touch, and he feels like he is about to vomit, because of all the people to have seen this moment. Claude Rose's smug face grins at them from the seat of his Valiant.

'What, just *one* word?' says Ross. 'How boring. The poor word will be all on its lonesome; maybe you should pair it with a challenge. Oh, wait, from what I've heard, you've already given one of those out today, haven't you?'

'Ross!' Orlando hisses, trying to get him to shut up, even though seeing him get all bitchy and defensive is sexy-as-all-hell, so Orlando kind of hopes Ross keeps giving it to Claude.

Claude glares. 'I would like nothing more than to challenge *you* Ross! You're a friend of Ben's, aren't you?'

'Listen guys,' says Orlando, 'we're in public. Either we go somewhere private to *discuss* this, or leave it alone. People are watching us.'

'Let them look,' cries Ross, not breaking eye contact with Claude.

A thin smile cracks the veneer of Claude's stony face as something behind them catches his eye. 'Don't worry about it,' he says, looking over Orlando's shoulder as Ben's panel van speeds past them. 'I'll let you boys get back to it; there goes *my* man.'

chapter thirteen

Street signs blur by Ben's window and he doesn't recognise the town in which he spent his life, for now, even the old and familiar is shiny and new. Faces glow at him as he drives by them and no one knows the secret that he carries around, like a note in his breast pocket, kept as close as possible to his heart. His unbelieving eyes flick from the road every few seconds, to perch like a butterfly on the new ring of his left hand, and then it flits away again as if carried up on a breeze of pure shock and delight that yes, the ring *is* real, and yes, the ring *is* there, and yes, it *is* a link to his wife, his wife, his wife!

Delia Rose – no wait, sorry, Delia *Starre* – is his wife, and their two families are now just *one* family, and he wants to grab the world by its shirt collar and scream this news into its shocked and wide-eyed face.

But Delia made him promise to wait.

There would be plenty of time, she said, to bask in the revelation of this new future. And her beautiful eyes had shimmered and she had smiled and said that for today she wanted to keep it secret, to hold it close, to keep it for only themselves, and tonight, oh tonight – a time that will surely not come fast enough – they will meet finally as husband and wife and join in body what they have already joined in name.

And once the marriage is consummated, they will walk downstairs hand in hand into the Rose's kitchen, and announce their union over coffee and toast.

Ben only hopes that this revelation does not fall at the same moment when Claude is in the process of spreading his breakfast with a knife, or pouring himself a scalding long black.

Looking at the blue sky, with its bright orb of daylight central and high, Ben urges the sun to go down, so that he can do the same thing with Delia while the chaperone of night watches on in perverted glee.

A horn blares behind him and he frowns into the rear vision mirror as Claude Rose's Valiant snarls and nips at his rear bumper.

Brilliant, Ben thinks. This is just what I need.

'Starre,' Claude growls through his open window, keeping his car level with Ben's as they continue to glide forward. 'I've only got one word for you: you're an asshole.'

'That's three words!' Ben says. 'And I'm not an asshole.'

There is a second rumble on the other side of Ben's

car, and he turns to see Ross pulling even with him as well.

'Hey!' Ross yells to Claude through the tunnel of Ben's front seat. 'I was talking to you, jerk!'

'Ross, just drop it,' Orlando hisses. 'Ben can handle his own fights.'

Geez, am I the only one watching the road here? Ben thinks, glancing from his friend and brother, to his new brother-in-law, and he slows to a stop at a set of green traffic lights.

'Claude,' Ben turns to him, 'whatever it is I have done to upset you, I'm sorry. I can't explain just yet, but you'll learn soon enough that I'm *not* your enemy. Not anymore.'

Claude shakes his head and his engine growls as he speaks. 'Don't give me that apology crap. You humiliated me last night, Starre!'

Ben frowns. 'What are you talking about? I didn't even see you last night. Just drop it, huh?'

'Ben!' Ross's shout drips with surprise. 'Don't let him talk to you like that.'

An impatient horn honks from behind them as the light changes from green to amber and blocked cars begin to line up.

'If you beat me, Starre,' says Claude, 'then I'll drop it.'

'Beat you?' Ben asks, even though he knows exactly what Claude means.

'Beat me!' The Valiant revs again.

'No way, man,' says Ben. 'I'm not racing you.'

'Chicken?'

The orange light changes into a bleary red eye, and the frustrated horn wails again from behind them.

'I can't explain right now,' Ben says again, 'but there is no feud between us anymore. It's over. So just forget it.'

'I'll race for Ben!' Ross yells. 'I'll be his second.'

'I got nothing against you.' Claude finally looks past Ben and acknowledges Ross. 'I want *him*.'

Ross's jaw sets like an angry pit bull. 'Well, you've got *me* instead.'

'Ross!' Orlando yells. 'What are you doing?'

'Yeah Ross, don't encourage him!' Ben says. 'No one is racing Claude.'

But Claude is smiling now. 'Fine!' he yells. 'Let's go.'

'Ross, don't do this!' Ben calls, but Ross isn't listening, his eyes are focused on the red light. 'Orlando, talk some sense into him, will you? Claude! Ross! You know Burgundy has put a ban on all this stupid racing stuff! Just stop! Please!'

And then the light blinks green. And then two engines scream. And then Ben watches the cars on either side of him launch away. And then he stamps his foot on the gas as well.

Not good, not good, not good! Damn you, Ross!

The only person Ben knows to be as stubborn as Claude Rose, is Ross Aylind, so to have these two face off in a stop-or-die challenge on a damn cliff top can only end in blood.

Ben's engine whines under the strain of sudden acceleration, and he chants, 'Come on, come on, come on!' as he tries to catch up to the cars ahead. A thin, cold, snake of dread curls in his gut, and it lounges there, heavy and deadly. 'Come *on!*' He begs the car to go faster as he watches the speedo climb slowly, slowly, slowly, and the cars ahead rise quickly, quickly, quickly, up the hill, over the crest, and disappear around the corner.

Ben rounds the straight just in time to see Claude and Ross turn sharply into the lookout and skid to twin stops at the cracked line in the tarmac. It's going to take him maybe thirty seconds to reach them, to pull his car in front of them and block them from killing themselves, and thirty seconds is plenty of time, hell, only twenty-five now, because this first stage of the challenge can last hours, as each driver waits for the other to go first.

A brown cloud of dust rises up from their wheels and begins to settle down around them, like the gown of a ghost, and Ben is only twenty seconds away now, and he hears someone laugh, and someone whoop, and tyres spin on gravel.

Both cars jump forward.

At first, it happens oh so slowly, as if Ben's stuttering heart has stopped the whole world, but then reality rushes in like a breath and everything happens all at once in a world too fast for even thought to keep up.

While Ross and Claude gain momentum, while their tyres spin and seek purchase and launch them from a standstill into a blur, Ben speeds into the lookout, keeps his foot on the accelerator and shoots right by them; he can still get ahead, he can still block their path, because this is Ross, because this is Orlando, because this is Claude, and if anything were to happen to either of them, then it would also be Ben's life that would be as broken as a falling body upon knife-sharp rocks.

The cliff edge races towards him much faster than he expects, as if *it* is driving at him while he drives at it, and he hears himself scream, and then he closes his eyes to it all, and stomps the brake, and turns the wheel, and just prays and prays and prays.

Ben slams against the side door as the car goes into a spin. Once again everything slows down and maybe it even stops for a heartbeat because suddenly he sees Delia's face and, really, what can possibly be wrong in his life if he can gaze upon the face of the woman he loves, the woman who loves him, the woman who belongs to him until death parts them, whenever that may be.

Dust rises up like a solid wall between Ben and the two onrushing vehicles.

Claude's car veers right, squeals in anger, and comes to a quick halt on the grassy picnic area.

Ross's car veers left, spins towards a shallow ditch, flips in the air once, twice, vomits Orlando from its belly, and lands upside-down. First, there is a sickening crunch of metal; second, a tinkling of raining glass; and third, the rough growl of Claude's engine as he guns it and sprays gravel and vanishes into the dust.

Ben's fingers slip on the handle and it takes him two tries before he can get his door to swing open like a shocked mouth. He falls out, lands on his knees, and for a moment he just stares from the crumpled and bloody form on the ground that he knows is his brother, to the smashed wreck of the car, inside which is his best friend.

Both of them are silent.

Dying?

Or already dead?

And to which one does he run first?

He closes his eyes and tries to summon Delia's face again, because she will bring clarity and reason and rightness back to his world. But all he can see now is blood.

He swallows a sob and an apology, and drops to his knees beside the body of his brother.

Orlando lays on his stomach, his face turned away, and Ben holds his breath and places a hand on Orlando's back and waits to see if it will rise and fall with the force of life.

'Orlando?' Ben whispers.

And when Orlando groans, and rolls over, Ben feels a sob rise from the bottom of his soul.

Orlando blinks. And says one word, which carries with it the weight of the entire earth. 'Ross?'

Ben scuttles like a spider towards the overturned car. One wheel spins lazily by his head as he drops to his belly and peers inside. 'Ross?' he calls. 'Ross!'

Ross still sits in his seat, his belt tight across his chest, hanging upside-down like a pig on a butcher's hook.

Ben shimmies in through the broken window and fumbles with the seatbelt. Maybe he shouldn't move him? What if there's a spinal injury? Ah, screw it all – Ross can live out his days in a damn wheelchair, so long as he does in fact *live* – because as Ben draws closer and sees Ross's gently parted lips, he also sees that no breath comes in or out of that rose-coloured doorway.

The click of the seatbelt echoes through Ben like a shot, and he sobs as Ross drops. And then he screams as Ross screams.

Ross's eyes open wide and fix on Ben, whose heart beats against a ribcage that is suddenly far too small to house an organ so swelled with relief.

'Ross!' he cries. 'You're okay, you're okay, you're okay.'

Something hot and wet drips on the back of his neck, and he looks up to see Ross's thigh held fast by the hungry metal teeth of the crumpled car.

Ben pulls but Ross pales even further and screams again.

'You're okay,' Ben says again. 'You're okay, you're okay, you're okay.'

But Ross blinks and shakes his head. 'Damn you both!'

'Is he hurt?' Orlando's face appears at the other side of the car, blocking the light and throwing Ross's snarling face into shadow.

'It's just a scratch,' Ross tells Orlando, 'but it's enough.'

'Call an ambulance,' says Ben.

Orlando fumbles his mobile from his pocket. 'It's smashed!' He turns and screams into the gathering crowd for someone to call an ambulance.

'You're okay,' Ben says again, 'I'm sure it's not that bad. They'll get you out of here. You're going to be fine.'

But Ross just shakes his head. 'It's not as deep as a well, or wide as a church door, but it's ... enough. It'll do. Oh, damn your families!' His jaw tightens. 'Why did you do that?' he says. 'Why did you come between us, Ben? I crashed because of *you*.'

'No!' Ben shakes his head, as if movement will prevent that accusation from sticking to him. 'No, I was trying to *protect* you.'

'Damn you both.' Ross's eyes roll back, and he whispers, 'you have *both* killed me.'

No. Ben shakes his head. No, not happening, not happening, not happening.

He had thought Claude couldn't be all that bad.

He'd thought, if Claude was born from the same genes as Delia then he couldn't be all that bad.

He'd thought, if this feud was over he could step seamlessly into a future with Delia.

But because of Delia – her beauty, her love – Ben had become weak, where he'd previously been as hard as steel. He'd looked for the good in someone he already knew had no trace of goodness. And in doing so, he had sacrificed Ross, someone he always knew to be pure goodness.

Ben grasps Ross's hand and vows that Claude Rose will pay for this. Whether he is Delia's brother or not, he will pay.

Orlando squeezes in beside them. He takes Ross's hand from Ben and presses it to his cheek so gently, so reverently, that Ben feels his eyes prickle with new tears.

'Orlando?' Ross whispers.

'I'm here,' he says.

'Tell me.'

Orlando chokes out a sound that could be either a laugh or a sob. Then he stares at Ross for forever and says, 'I like you.'

Ross gives a weak smile. 'Guess we should've gone to my place after all.'

'Help is coming, okay,' Orlando whispers. 'You hold on. Please, hold on.' He squeezes Ross's hand, and then lets out a soft, 'No.'

Ben follows his brother's gaze. He sees Orlando squeeze again, he sees that Ross does not squeeze back, and he too lets out a soft, 'No.'

Orlando looks up. 'Ben,' he cries. 'Do something!'

His little brother, with his eyes huge and wet and pleading. His little brother, whom he is supposed to watch over and protect. His little brother, who is, yet again, losing something, because of him. Something Ben has been waiting for his little brother to find for such a long time.

'Do something!' Orlando begs.

So Ben nods, and crawls out of the car, and stands.

He will do something because Claude is alive and triumphant, while Ross hangs broken in an overturned car.

He will do something because he needs to make Claude pay.

He will do something because if he can blame Claude, then he will no longer have to blame himself.

His feet punch and punch and punch the gravel as he runs to his van, and he barely registers Orlando's words, 'Where are you going? You can't leave? Don't leave me! Ben!'

But first his anger drowns Orlando out, and then his engine drowns Orlando out, and then those words are behind Ben as he flies down the hill, and he finds Claude so fast he must have been drawn to him by fate.

At a set of lights, Claude's brakes glow like demon eyes above the grinning chrome bumper.

'Claude!' Ben's voice is high and unrecognisable as he rams his van straight into the smug, smiling rear end of the car.

Glass falls with a satisfying tinkle onto the road as those demon eyes are blinded.

Doors fly open.

The two men stand, chest to chest, in the middle of the street.

Ben shoves Claude and screams right into his face. 'Ross's soul hovers just above our heads, waiting for you to keep him company.' He shoves again.

Claude doesn't shove back, he just stumbles and waits for the next shove.

'Either you,' Ben shoves, 'or me,' Ben shoves, 'or both,' Ben shoves, 'will go with him!'

'On green, then,' says Claude, in an contrastingly calm voice. He steps away and slides into his car.

Ben pulls his van into the right lane, but it doesn't matter because there is hardly any oncoming traffic on this road. He pulls alongside Claude, and they stare together at the red light. As each second ticks closer to green, and to the end of all this, the air thickens in his throat and his heart throbs so hard his entire body jolts in rhythm. *Lub-dub. Lub-dub. Lub-dub.*

Green.

Ben's foot presses the pedal to the floor and the engine whines, pleadingly, but he does not let up, and he keeps pace with Claude, and he doesn't care about common sense anymore. He is speeding down a two-way street on the wrong side of the road, and who cares? He is racing against Claude Rose, the unbeatable racer, and who cares? This is incredibly stupid and dangerous and exhilarating and who the hell cares?

Their cars remain level as they speed along the straight, around a bend, and another bend, and into another straight where, even though Ben's van begins to shudder with effort, it pulls ahead just enough to swerve in front of Claude, and into the lead.

Ben turns left down a skinny street, knowing that Claude has no choice now but to follow him onto this winding cliff road.

On his left is a wall of rock and shrubs that rises up into the sky. On his right is nothing but bright sky, heaven, and a steep drop onto sharp rocks below.

Leaning forward, he squints up through the windscreen to see above the jagged edge of the lookout where a flashing blue and red light pulses. With every strobe of those beacons, Ben's heart thumps harder and louder, chanting: *Ross, Ross, Ross. I'm sorry, I'm sorry, I'm sorry. Make him pay, make him pay, make him pay.*

Only Ben is no longer sure if he is seeking vengeance against Claude Rose, or against himself.

chapter fourteen

Claude bites down on a laugh as Ben's peace-of-crap van cuts him off. He slams the brakes hard so he doesn't run right up the douche's ass.

'Well,' he mumbles, 'look who finally grew some balls!' Claude spins the wheel and shouts, 'Come on, baby!' as he shoots forward the way a *real* car should, passing Ben so easily the loser might as well be parked.

As he overtakes Ben, Claude sees a glimmer of chrome flash in the distance, then disappear around an oncoming bend so quickly he's not even sure if it was really there.

Still, his stomach clenches like a fist and his skin prickles with sweat. Instinct screams in his ear to brake and pull back in behind Ben, but Claude knows he still has time. He just needs to get a little further ahead to get in front and leave that creep crying in his dust cloud.

Claude presses his foot down harder on the accelerator – so hard his calf muscle cramps – but the pedal is already to the floor, and he glances sideways at Ben, who stares with narrowed eyes at the winding road.

When he turns forward again, Claude sees a God damn oncoming truck – all polished chrome and snarling grille – rounding the bend up ahead.

Its horn blares a warning to get of his damn way, but Claude is almost there, almost there, almost there.

The truck is closing in, and Claude is not passing Ben fast enough, and if he doesn't pull back now, right now, he's going to end twitching like a bug on that truck's windscreen.

Claude hisses a swear, and punches the steering wheel, and taps the brake, and sees Ben shoot out ahead, which is okay, because he can still catch him on the straight.

The truck blares its horn again, and flashes its lights.

'Yeah, yeah, I'm moving!' Claude yells.

But just as he drops back far enough to swing over behind Ben, the van's brake lights flare red.

Ben drops back level with Claude.

And Claude is blocked in, pinned between Ben's van on the left and the metal safety rail on the right, and he is suddenly chilled in the shadow of the almighty truck as it blares its horn again, and Claude doesn't know which is louder: that damn horn, or the shocked silence of his own impending death.

chapter fifteen

Ben never imagines anything can be so loud. The noise of the crash shudders through his bones; that echo will resound within him forever.

By the time Ben's van stops, Claude is gone from sight, and the truck's brakes are squealing and smoking down the road, and Ben's mind is suddenly clear, so damn clear that he can see every single crack and scratch that marks him.

And in that moment of clarity, I return to him. But of course now my words are no longer a prediction, or a warning. Now, my words are the truth.

In Ben's mind, he hears my voice as crystal-real as it had been in the moment I spoke to him: *Dripping fangs of guilt will pierce your soul, and vengeance-seeking venom infect your mind. More strength to smile than to respond in kind.*

I had been right. He knows this now.

He has done exactly as I said he would: he sought

vengeance, because he was too weak to stand back and smile and just let things be.

And now?

Oh, Christ. Now ...

The truck driver is out and running to the edge and peering over and climbing down.

Above Ben, at the lookout, a crowd points down at him. People are shouting into phones or taking pictures, and surely Burgundy will be there in minutes.

He'll be in a jail cell before the next hour has ticked over.

And Delia, who is waiting to greet her new husband, will instead open her door to the spectre of Death, who has stolen away her brother.

Why did he let his anger take over? He was such an idiot! Why had he not listened to me? I told him this was going to happen, I had given him the knowledge of foresight that others would have killed for, and still he had let this happen.

But then, had he *let* this happen? Or, did he have no choice?

The wail of sirens pierces Ben's brain and, as he sends out a prayer to Delia for forgiveness, he puts his foot to the floor, accelerating away along the path of fate once again.

chapter sixteen

The ambulance wails out of the lookout with Ross inside; the desperate scream of that siren, its pitch and fall, sounds to Orlando exactly like disbelief.

Ross, whom he has loved from afar for years.

Ross, who fell in love with Ben, and remained by his side even with a constant weight of heartbreak dragging him down.

Ross, who finally admitted feelings for Orlando.

Ross, who was forced into a situation where he'd had to choose between his new love and his old one.

And Ross, who is now, as a result of that choice, being spirited away.

Orlando's fists clench and he blinks at tears.

Yet again, Ben has taken away the one thing Orlando wants. And why? What the hell does Ben care anyway? He made it clear he wasn't interested in Ross, that the only one who mattered to him was this precious Olivia; Ben didn't even notice the torture Ross had gone through watching the man he couldn't have pine after a woman that didn't want him. Ben didn't notice anyone but himself. Until, that is, Ross had finally blinked away from Ben's moon-bright hair and sky-bright eyes, and had instead seen the little brother of the wonderful Benedick Starre. Finally, Orlando was happy, but for some reason, Ben stepped in to destroy that happiness. Ben doesn't want Ross, but doesn't want anyone else to have him, either, is that it? And not just *anyone* else, his God damned *brother*!

Or perhaps, Orlando thinks, that is exactly the point. It is acceptable for Ben's best friend to be a homosexual, but not his own brother.

A second siren rises in volume as Burgundy's police cruiser pulls up, followed by Orlando's parents, and then the Roses.

Oh, no. Here we go again.

Standing at the edge of the lookout, Orlando can see down to where Claude's wrecked car glints in the sun. An ambulance pulls up to where Claude's car smashed through the metal barrier, and two orderlies rush down the cliff face.

Imogen Rose grips the lookout fence for support, stares down at her son's mangled car, and gasps, 'My boy! My boy! No!'

Shepherd Rose wraps an arm around his wife and draws her into his chest where she sobs violently.

'What happened here?' barks Burgundy at the crowd of wide-eyed onlookers.

Orlando keeps his eyes focused over the edge and says nothing.

'Burgundy!' Imogen Rose screeches, lifting her face from her husband's chest. 'You make that Starre boy pay for this!'

The police officer steps forward. 'Orlando?' he says, softly. 'What exactly happened here? Who started this?'

Orlando clears his throat and he wants to say that it's all his brother's fault, that Ben screwed up everything for everyone, and that he should be taken away forever, taken out of their lives so that maybe it will be *his* turn to be the favourite son. But instead, Orlando whispers, 'It was Claude. He wanted Ben to race him, but Ben tried to *stop* it. He tried to make Claude see how trivial this rivalry is, and reminded him of your warning. But Claude wouldn't listen, wouldn't give up, and then ...' He stops and takes a breath, preparing to feel the dead weight of pain on his tongue, 'and then *Ross* stepped in, and said he'd take Ben's place in the race. I think Ben tried to get between them, to stop them both, but Ross lost control of his car and crashed. We thought he was dead.' Orlando's throat closes and he coughs to clear it. 'Ben kind of lost it; he shot off after Claude, and Claude ended up down there.' Orlando nods towards the cliff edge.

Imogen Rose reels away from her husband and storms forward, pointing at Orlando with perfectly manicured fingernails. 'He is Ben's brother; of course he'll say that Claude started it. Please, Sergeant, give me some justice for what's happened to my son! Ben must pay!'

Burgundy turns to her and narrows his eyes into slits. 'And what about justice for poor Ross Aylind, which was caused by *your son?*' A ball of white frothy spit forms in the corner of Burgundy's grimacing mouth. 'Who should pay for *that?*'

'Not Ben, sir.' Morgan Starre steps forward, raising a hand as if holding up a stop sign. 'He's Ross's best friend; as far as he is concerned, Claude killed him, so he was carrying out a sentence that justice would have carried out anyway.'

'What?' Imogen's eyes bulge at him. 'By forcing his car off a cliff! That's not *justice*, Morgan!'

'No.' Burgundy nods once, briskly. 'And for that Ben *will* be punished. He is not to come within one hundred kilometres of this town's boundary. Ever again.'

'That's *all?*' yells Imogen. 'You're not going to arrest Ben? Charge him? Jail him?'

'From what I've heard,' Burgundy says, 'Ben was not the one driving erratically on the wrong side of the road! I told you I'd be enforcing this new law and, by God, I meant it. Ross was a good friend of mine, and look what has happened to him because of your petty feuding. No amount of pleading, excuses, tears, or prayers from any of you will change my mind on this: if Ben is *found* in this town again, he *will* be arrested and jailed immediately.'

With a sob, Imogen Rose lets her husband lead her back to their car, and they drive away, heading towards the hospital to be with Claude.

Orlando wonders where Ross is right this second. He wonders if he is alone. And he wonders why the hell he is still standing here.

Ross may only have few precious moments left on this earth and Orlando wants to spend them holding his hand. And so what if the town finds out? And so what if his father finds out? Morgan Starre is already disappointed that his second son is not as perfect as his first; what will more disappointment matter?

'Take me to the hospital, Dad.' Orlando strides with a purpose now towards his parents' car. 'I need to be with Ross.'

'They won't let you in, son,' says Morgan. 'Only family will be allowed in to see him. Only his loved ones.'

Orlando's jaw sets and he stares into his father's eyes. 'Then they will have to let *me* in. Because I love him. And he loves me. And I am gay. And I don't care what you think about that.'

Morgan and Desdemona Starre both stare at their son for a heavy beat of time before his mother wipes at a tear, and his father places both his hands on Orlando's shoulders, holding him steady and still. 'Son.' But Morgan's voice breaks and he doesn't finish his sentence. He just nods, blinks his suddenly watery eyes, and ushers Orlando to the car.

As they speed out of the lookout, Orlando can see that his mother is smiling.

Then Morgan meets his eyes in the rear-view mirror and says, 'I'm proud of you.'

His father says these words so softly that Orlando barely hears them, yet they resonate within his bones like the chime of a great bell, echoing and sustaining that perfect note forever.

'And I want you to know,' Morgan continues, 'that whatever happens in the coming days, son, no matter what, you're not alone in this. Your mother and I are here for you. Always.'

The car pulls up at the doors to the hospital and Desdemona nods towards them. 'Now you get in there,' she says. 'Ross is waiting for you.'

chapter seventeen

Delia can barely keep her skin from bursting open in excitement. She is as happy as the day is long. And this day is as long as forever.

Staring through her bedroom window, she watches the slow, lazy sun, high in the sky, taunting her with its brightness.

Move faster, damn you!

Why can't she just fasten a team of horses to the sun, and they can gallop straight to the western horizon, drawing with them the shade of night and the promise of fulfilment.

There is a sudden surge in her belly and between her legs as she thinks of what darkness will bring tonight: the secrecy, the thrill of the taboo with her naïve family hovering somewhere on the other side of these thin walls, all unaware that she is single-handedly changing the course of their lives for the better.

'You're welcome,' she whispers, and lets out a laugh.

Thinking again of the walls, and the way she often hears conversations easily through the plaster, she wonders if her husband is a silent lover. That delicious surge pulses again, accompanied by a fierce burning in her cheeks.

I'm blushing? She presses a hand to her hot face. He's not even here yet and I'm blushing? How bad will I glow once he is naked and waiting in my bed?

This is going to be a disaster. Surely, Ben Starre has been with plenty of women, has had *experienced* lovers in his bed, and now ... her. A blushing bride. Literally. A shy little virgin who has absolutely no idea what the hell she is doing, and he is going to know, and oh God, this is going to be a disaster!

Maybe that's why she suggested they meet at night, so at least he wouldn't see her blushing?

She groans and rolls over and presses her face into the pillow. For a moment, it is as dark as night and she sees him, like she does whenever she shuts her eyes. He is there: his face a constellation of stars that would create a sky so lovely that everyone who gazed up at it would fall in the love with night's brilliance, and forget all about the ostentatious and garish beauty of the sun. But he is *hers*. This man whose face has the power to entrance all who look upon him is *her* husband.

Her *husband*.

She laughs in amazement at the sheer strangeness of that word, and turns the golden ring, the *wedding* ring, on her finger. She feels slightly cheated, slightly ripped off, like she's just purchased a lavish mansion and holds the keys in her palm, but hasn't yet been allowed inside its doors.

Heavy footsteps echo in the hall, growing louder, closer, and her heart catches.

But then she relaxes because it wouldn't be *him*.

Would it?

No, not yet. Not while the sun is still teasingly high in the sky.

Unless he somehow found out that she is home alone.

She stands and stares at the door and holds her breath, and when the knob turns and the door opens, and Katherine flows in on a river of tears, at first Delia lets out her breath in a surge of disappointment and then in a flush of nervous relief and then in a gasp of trepidation. 'What's wrong?'

'There's been an accident,' Katherine whispers, sinking onto the bed. 'He's in hospital. Oh, Delia. It looks serious.'

'No.' Delia's one single syllable cracks like glass under the weight of Katherine's words.

'I'm so sorry,' says Katherine. 'Oh, Ben! Whoever would have thought ... Ben ...'

'No,' Delia says again, and shakes her head because this isn't fair; just when she's finally found him, he gets taken away before she even has a chance to love him.

Can fate really be so cruel? 'What ...' she swallows. 'What happened?'

'I don't know.' Katherine takes a breath and wipes her eyes. 'But I saw the wreck. I saw his body; it was so pale! Like ashes. And there was so much blood.'

'It was a race?' Delia's chest lurches. A sting. An ache. Her heart splits in half; she feels it ripping, snapping, fibre by fibre, *plink plink plink*. How can she possibly live out the rest of her years alone, without him by her side? Her soul mate. Her one. Her husband.

She closes her eyes tight, and as she sees his face again the pain in her chest flares bright and she wishes for it to seize her, to kill her, to end her, if he has been ended too.

'I mean, Claude ... he's like a brother to me!' Katherine is sobbing again. 'Oh, if he dies ...'

'What?' Delia whispers, shaking her head in disbelief now. 'Ben's on the brink of death, *and* Claude, too?'

She can't believe it. It's just too horrible to even contemplate. Her beautiful brother, and her beautiful husband? What's the point in living if *both* of them are gone?

Katherine stares. Then she frowns. 'Claude is in hospital. And Ben? Ben is not hurt; he is the one who caused the crash. He is gone.'

The treaty, Delia thinks and her breath hitches in her throat. Did Ben really harm her own brother? Why would he do something like that? They are supposed to be ending this feud once and for all. Hasn't that been the whole point? Love conquering all?

Her jaw clenches and she squeezes her eyes closed on reality, glaring instead into Ben's face as it rises like a moon in her imagination. She stares at his beauty and wonders if she has been completely fooled. She feels as if she's bent down to press her face into a glorious flower only to have a snake dart out and sink fangs into her cheek, or as if she's discovered the most beautiful cave, when suddenly a dragon's head appears with hungry yellow eyes. She wonders if he, like a murderous crow disguised with the white feathers of a dove, has deceived her, tricked her, betrayed her? As if that had been his plan all along.

Her skin burns and she wants to peel it from her bones, to be unrecognisable as the idiot she is.

How could someone she loves so much turn out to be so horrible as to hurt her own brother?

'That son of a bitch!' Katherine growls. 'He fled, but I hope they find him; I hope he gets what he deserves!'

'Don't you dare talk about him like that!' Delia rounds on her, and Katherine flinches backwards from the heat of her sudden anger, and God it feels so good to direct that hot hatred out at someone, at anyone, rather than sizzling up her own internal organs.

Katherine gapes. 'You're going to *defend* the man who has put your brother in a critical condition?'

'He's still my *husband!*' Delia spits out the words of

defence, even though Katherine said exactly what Delia had been thinking only moments before.

But *Katherine* doesn't love Ben.

Delia does.

Delia *does*.

Delia *loves* him.

No matter what he has done, she bloody loves him. As much as she may not want to, she loves him. So therefore, she is the only one allowed to think badly of him, thank you very much.

'Ben is not the only one responsible,' Delia says. 'They were both racing, weren't they? So, it was an accident; it could easily have been Ben injured, and Claude on the run from the cops.'

Tears sting her eyes in a blistering and unexpected surge of happiness. Of relief. Because Ben is all right. *Not* injured. *Not* dead. She slashes at these new tears of joy, which even as they spill over and salt Delia in their liquid streams of joy, also stain her in renewed sorrow, because she understands what this means now: Ben must leave town.

And those two words, *leave town*, hurt Delia's heart more than ten thousand critically injured brothers. Those combined pains – Claude's accident, and Ben's leaving – fuse together and grow like a cancer.

Misery loves company.

Christ, why doesn't Katherine just say that her

mother is dead, too? And her father? And her damn cat! They might as well all be taken from her.

'Where's Mum and Dad?' Delia ask.

'They're with Claude at the hospital. Come on, I'll drive you.' Katherine stands and reaches for Delia's hand.

'No.' Delia walks past her to the door. 'I have to find Ben first.'

'You can't be serious,' says Katherine.

'He needs me right now.'

'No, your parents need you right now. Claude needs you right now. You should be at the hospital with them.'

Katherine is right. Delia knows she's right. What if Claude doesn't make it? But she shakes her head before that thought has a chance to take root.

'Fine,' Delia says, 'you go.'

'What?'

'Give him this.' Delia slips her wedding ring from her finger. 'Tell him to meet me tonight, as planned, so he can give the ring back to me again. I'll have my things packed and ready.'

Katherine doesn't take the ring. She just blinks. 'You're going to *leave*?'

'I don't have any other choice!'

'Your brother has just been in a horrible car accident and you're going to run out on your family when they need the most support?'

'Katherine, just give him the damn message!'

But she sits down on the end of the bed and stares at

Delia, stricken, as if looking at a ghost. 'Oh, Delia. I'm so scared for you. I've been trying to ignore all these signs, but I can't ignore them now. Jesus, don't you see? It's all true. The prophecy, everything the gypsy lady said, it's all coming true, and I'm scared. I'm so scared I'm going to lose *you* next.'

'Lose me?' Seeing her best friend crumpling right before her eyes dissolves all the anger and frustration Delia felt a second before. 'I'll keep in touch every day,' she says, sitting on the bed. 'Just because I'll be in a different town means nothing, you know that. Hell, we've always stayed close while I was away at school, so how is this any different?'

'Because,' Katherine whispers, 'you were alive.'

'Oh, come on.' Delia laughs. 'I am not going to kill myself, okay? I promise.'

'But you don't have any control over this! Not anymore. The prophecy, or destiny, or whatever, is the one in charge now.'

'The definition of killing yourself means that you and you alone are the one in control of whether or not it happens. It would be my decision and I'm telling you now that I will not commit suicide.'

'I've heard that before,' Katherine mutters.

'And what is that supposed to mean?' Delia crosses her arms over her chest to muffle the loud and sudden booming of her heart. 'You know that was an accident.'

'An accident? You mean you cut yourself while shaving your wrist?'

Delia's eyes prickle with guilt. She holds her arms behind her back, even though she knows her long sleeve hides the thin silver line that slashes her left forearm. 'I'm a different person than I was then.'

'Fine.' Katherine stands and tucks the wedding ring into her jeans pocket. 'It's your funeral.' She leaves the room and doesn't look back, but those words hover around Delia as if they are tangible winged creatures.

It's your funeral.

She shrinks away from them, and takes a steadying breath before she too leaves the room, trapping Katherine's prophecy behind the bedroom door so it can not follow her. So it can not convince her to change her mind.

It's your funeral.

Delia flies down the stairs, racing now against a new entity that she can not see, yet knows is only a few steps behind, and gaining on her with every passing second.

As she snatches up her keys, she wonders how fast she will have to drive in order to outrun time itself.

chapter eighteen

Puck closes his front door and leans back against the stained window. The length of the corridor dances with coloured light. Coming home to this welcoming rainbow usually fills him with bright happiness. But not now. Not today.

Instead, an armour of sadness closes over his skin, an armour too tough for the calming influence of reds and yellows and blues to penetrate.

'Christ, Ben,' he calls out. 'This day started out on such a high, right here within these walls. New love. The promise of peace. The ability to change lives. How could things have dragged down so fiercely, so quickly?' Shaking his head, he enters the lounge and folds to the floor with his back against the sofa. 'How many times have I told you that it takes a stronger man to walk away, than to stand and fight? How many damn times!'

Sighing, Puck reaches beneath the couch. In the dark depths, his fingers tap around until they hit cool solid metal. He slides out a small box and places it between his legs, opens the lid, and lets the sweet smell of marijuana waft out and engulf him. Now *this* calming influence, he knows, can easily penetrate the armour of sadness with a promise of coming peace.

Rolling the herb between his fingers, he licks the papers, smooths them down, and then holds the joint above his head. 'I know you're here, man!' he calls out. 'Come out, and get some of this into you; it'll help put things in perspective. Things aren't always as bad as they seem, you know? Even though you may as well have married Disaster this morning, instead of Delia Rose.'

Puck waits maybe thirty seconds before a tear-stained Ben emerges from the hallway like an apparition.

'How'd you know I was here?' he croaks.

'Where else would you be?'

'What happened? Is Claude alive? What did Burgundy say?' Ben crawls over on his hands and knees, and takes the joint in shaking fingers, like a sinner reaching for absolution.

'Claude's in a critical condition, but they think he'll make it.' Puck hands over a lighter.

Ben's face glows orange as he inhales. 'And,' he says, blowing out smoke, 'what about Burgundy?'

Puck pauses and says nothing.

'What did he say?' Ben asks.

'Just remember that it could be worse, dude.'

'What did he say?' Ben says again.

Puck takes a breath and then speaks the words quickly, as if they have no more meaning than a comment on the weather. 'You can't be within one hundred kilometres of the town's border.'

'I've been *exiled*?' The joint falls from Ben's fingers. 'Is that legal?' he gasps. 'Can he do that?'

'Apparently so.' Puck snatches the cigarette up before it singes the carpet.

'Oh! I've been banished,' he sobs. 'I'd rather be sent to jail than forced to leave here. Are you sure that's what he said? Maybe you misheard him?'

'Nope.' Puck inhales deeply, pulling the sweet smoke into his chest. 'So, you can't come near here anymore.' He shrugs. 'So what? You can start a new life somewhere else. There's a big wide world out there.'

'A *new* life?' Ben shouts. 'There is no life for me outside this town!'

'You don't get it, do you?' Puck's breath clouds around them both like despair. 'Burgundy has every right to send you to prison! If that is really what you'd prefer, I can arrange for that. Shit, man. If Claude dies, it's manslaughter, do you dig? This is serious shit. But Burgundy understands that you acted irrationally; he's giving you a second chance because you're Ross's friend.'

'Ross?' Ben's face pales, but then he shakes his head as if he can't bear to think of his friend right now. 'Easy on me? This is torture!' He stands, pacing back and forwards.

'My life is meant to be here, with Delia, and now every cat, dog, mouse, everything else, every*one* else will be able to see her but me! Disease-ridden *flies* are luckier than I am, for God's sake! They can land on her, touch her skin, but not me because I've been freaking banished!' He wipes tears off his cheek with his sleeve. 'And you reckon it could have been *worse?*'

'Listen to me, you idiot!' Puck's words explode from him. 'You're not thinking about this in the right way.'

'The *right* way? I don't want to hear any of your hippie philosophy crap right now, Puck! You can't talk about something you're not feeling! If you were in love with Delia, if you had been married to her for only a few short hours, if you had possibly killed her brother, and if you were now forced to run away and leave your new wife behind, *then* you could comment on how I feel!' His knees buckle and he sinks to the floor, head in hands, and his words now come in a whisper. 'But you can't possibly feel what I feel, so you don't have the right to philosophise to me right now.'

'Why don't you just ask her to go with you?' Puck says.

Ben's head rocks back and forth, and his voice is muffled by his hands. 'She won't want me now. Not after what I did. It's over, man. It's all over.'

A loud knocking on the front door scares the gosh-darn crap out of Puck. Springing up, he rushes to the window. 'Get up!' he hisses. 'Someone's here; you got to hide, man.'

'Why?' Ben wails. 'What's the point?'

The knocker raps again, louder this time.

'Who is it?' Puck calls as normally, and as not-stoned as he can, while stuffing his grass and papers back into the tin. He grinds the joint into the ashtray and glares at his stupid-ass friend. 'Ben, get up! You'll be arrested,' he whispers, and then yells out, 'Just a minute!' Puck tries to physically lift Ben off the floor. 'Stand up! Go hide in the study, will you?'

On the third and even more insistent knocking, he gives up and leaves Ben crumpled on the floor. 'Who is it? What do you want?'

'It's Katherine. I'm Delia Rose's friend.'

Puck opens the door to see the girl who had worn the pink bunny slippers during that morning's ceremony, back when everything had still been perfect.

'Do you know where he is?' she asks.

'Whoever do you mean?' Puck says.

Katherine rolls her eyes. 'Don't give me that B.S., Puck. Ben effing Starre! Where is he?'

Puck hesitates, staring at this fierce woman's wide, bugged-out eyes.

She sighs. 'I have something for him.'

For a second, Puck wonders if she conceals some kind of weapon in her coat. What could possibly happen if he does let her inside? But then, would it look even worse if he didn't let her in? If Ben wasn't here, then what reason would he have to refuse her entry into the house? By not letting her in, she would surely guess that Ben was in fact hiding here, that Puck was harbouring a fugitive, and she could have Burgundy on his doorstep in minutes.

But then, she is Delia's friend. And he saw the way that girl looked at Ben today; love cannot be plucked out as easily as a flower from soil. Surely not.

Puck opens the door and steps back. 'He's crying like a girl on my lounge room floor.'

'So is Delia,' Katherine says. 'Although she *is* a girl.' She stops in the lounge doorway and takes in the image of Ben, gazing up, tear-stained and pathetic on the very same shag rug upon which he and Delia had exchanged vows mere hours ago.

'Katherine?' Ben slowly unfolds himself. 'How is Delia? Does she hate me for what I've done to her brother? Where is she? How is she? Is it over between us?'

'Delia is heartbroken.' She speaks in a slow, controlled voice. 'She's in tears over her brother. And, for reasons I do not understand, she's in tears over you. Ben Starre, I wish I could punch you in the throat and tell you to leave my best friend alone. In fact, that is just what I came here to say to you. To tell you she never wants to see you again.' She swallows and stands a little taller. 'Here.'

When she digs her hand into her pocket, Puck tenses, hoping she is not about to pull out a knife and stab Ben right there on his expensive shag rug. But when she opens her fist, a ring gleams in the centre of her palm.

Ben scrambles like a crab away from this symbol of marriage, as if Katherine is in fact holding a knife out towards him.

'She told me to give this to you,' spits Katherine. She closes her eyes as she speaks the next few words, as if she cannot bear to witness them coming from her own lips. 'You can give it back to her tonight. She'll have her bags packed and ready to go with you.'

'What?' Ben gasps.

'You see!' Puck steps forward and pulls Ben to his feet. 'Now stop being so bloody dramatic! Stop crying; be a man! Delia still loves you; be grateful. What happened with Claude was an accident – it could easily have been you in his place; be grateful. Your punishment has been lightened; be grateful. You're not seeing this in the positive; instead you're acting like a spoiled brat, pouting, and not being *grateful* for what you have. Get yourself cleaned up, then go and get your wife.'

Walking over to a large cabinet, Puck pulls out a drawer and rifles through a whole lot of useless crap he's shoved in there, until, 'Aha!' he holds up a set of keys and jangles them in the air. Scribbling an address down on a piece of paper, he hands both the paper and keys to Ben. 'Here, I own a holiday house. It's yours for as long as you need it. Wait there until you hear from me. In the meantime, I'll get everything straightened out: I'll broadcast your love and marriage to both your parents, who will be forced, then, to bury their grudges against one another. Assuming Claude recovers, I'll talk to Burgundy, explain everything. Hopefully he'll lift your sentence, and then you and Delia can both return, and live your lives in the manner you were meant to: happily ever after. Trust me, man, I'll take care of everything.'

'Yeah, right,' Katherine huffs in the doorway.

Puck turns to her. 'Go tell Delia that Ben is on his way.'

'Marvellous.' She throws the ring on the rug at Ben's feet, and whirls from the room, muttering, 'Gee, I didn't know *that* was going to happen!' and she slams the front door behind her with the force of a gunshot.

In the middle of the lounge, Ben kneels and picks up the ring with such gentleness, as if it were a baby bird fallen from a nest. As he slips the band on his little finger, beside his own wedding ring, he looks up at Puck and smiles.

In that instant, with Ben's smile illuminating the room, Puck believes that he really *can* live up to the promises he made, that it *will* all work out in the end. That peace will, as he had originally hoped, be restored to this town.

'It's getting late,' Puck says. 'You'd better go.'

'I wish we could have a better goodbye,' Ben says, nodding towards the hidden metal box beneath the sofa.

'How about we postpone it,' says Puck. 'We'll have a proper *welcome home* instead.'

Ben nods and reaches for Puck's hand to shake, but Puck grabs it and pull his friend in for a hug. A goodbye of sorts. Just in case the small kernel of doubt in his gut turns out to be right.

chapter nineteen

The image of his son comes in and out of focus, and Shepherd Rose is grateful for his tears; they momentarily lessen the severity of his child's injuries behind a salty veil of hope. Claude's skin is milk pale in the few places where it's not swollen and purple. His body, visible only as a hulky shape beneath the pale blue blanket, seems small, birdlike.

Shepherd has never seen him so vulnerable. Even as a newborn, this boy had given off an aura of strength. And now, he is just ... this ... thing. Fragile as a cracked egg.

As he stares down at his boy, and as his vision blurs again at the edges, Shepherd wonders what else he is unable to see in this room. Are there shimmering spectres of loved ones at the foot of Claude's bed, waiting to take him home? Or is the black-shrouded form of Death standing vigil, waiting to take Claude someplace else?

The skin at the base of his neck prickles and he rubs a

hand over it, and then he jumps out of his God damned skin as a voice speaks softly in his ear: 'How is he?'

'Christ!' Shepherd mutters, as he turns to face Guy Shylock. 'You scared the life out of me.' And then, as the heat of those words rises around them both like steam, Shepherd clears his throat. 'If he makes it through the night, then he should be out of the woods. But they say the next few hours will be touch and go.'

Guy offers a smile and squeezes Shepherd's shoulder. 'He'll pull through. He's one tough son of a bitch.'

'Yeah.' Shepherd coughs to clear a passage for his words. 'You just missed Delia; she left about ten minutes ago.'

'Oh.' Guy presses his lips together in disappointment. 'That's okay. How is she holding up?'

'She's not taking it well at all,' says Shepherd. 'The whole time she was here, she just sat there looking at his face, shaking her head like she couldn't believe what she was seeing. She'd open her mouth to say something, but then simply close it again. To be honest, Guy, I'm worried. It scares me when she gets all quiet like this. That's what she was like before she ... had her accident.'

Guy blinks and hesitates as if the shutters of his eyelids show him scenes he'd rather not see. 'And Imogen?' He walks around the other side of the bed and leans down, studying Claude's face. 'How is she coping?'

'She's gone to get coffee. She keeps making excuses to leave the room.'

Lowering himself into a chair beside the bed, Guy sighs, 'Listen, Shepherd, I hate to bring this up at a time like this, but this is a *private* hospital.'

'So?' Shepherd narrows his eyes. 'My son deserves the best!'

'But ... it's expensive.'

'And that's why it's the best.'

'Yes, but, how are you planning on *paying* for it?' Guy leans forward, resting his elbows on his knees. 'You're broke.'

'What other choice have I got?' Shepherd hisses. 'If I check him into the *public* hospital, people will wonder why. *Imogen* will wonder why.'

Shepherd drops onto a second chair as the weight of his burden is suddenly too heavy to carry for another moment longer. 'I don't know,' he says. 'I could take out another loan on the business but I need Imogen's signature for that.'

Guy holds up a gentle hand, halting Shepherd with hope. 'That's why I came to see you. I've got a proposition for you: I'll give you the money to get back on your feet, get out of debt. You don't even have to pay me back, and no one ever has to know about it.'

'Why?' Shepherd asks. 'Why would you do that for me?'

'Well,' he smiles, 'I do have one condition.'

'Anything.' Shepherd swallows. 'Just name it and it's yours.'

'Delia.'

Shepherd frowns at him. 'Haven't we already had this conversation?'

'We're perfect for each other, sir. I think she just needs someone she loves, someone she trusts, to make her realise that.'

'Someone like me?'

Guy nods.

But Shepherd knows this is hopeless. His daughter is as stubborn as her brother when it comes to what she wants, or doesn't want. Guy had his shot with Delia last night and obviously he failed to make a lasting impression. Delia doesn't give second chances. She believes in fate and love at first sight and all that romantic crap, so if she didn't want Guy after last night, then there is not much at all that Shepherd could possibly do to change her mind.

Unless ...

His stomach churns at the thought. Yet his heart speeds up with the thrill of his only possible salvation. Shepherd closes his eyes. 'All right.'

'Really?' A wide grin cracks Guy's handsome face. 'You think she'll agree?'

'She'll agree,' says Shepherd.

She'll agree, he thinks, because she'll see there's no other option.

Delia will always, *always* do what is best for the ones

she loves. Even when those same loved ones do not do what is best for her.

Taking a breath, Shepherd feels his chest expand as a weight lifts from his bones. But as he exhales, a new weight settles there, heavier than the first, as black and unyielding as the cloak of Death itself.

chapter twenty

The sun bends down low enough now to kiss the lips of the horizon, making the blue cheeks of the sky blush pink.

Delia hears a scrabbling on the boughs of the tree above, and Ben drops out of heaven to land at her feet like a gift, and she can't breathe.

Because this man, whose kisses she yearns for more than breath, whose soul she doesn't know how to untangle from her own, and whose eyes are shot through with regret, is the same man who almost killed her brother.

Because this man, whose heart beats so loud she feels it through the soles of her shoes, and whose skin pulls her forward like they are both made of magnets, and whose mouth can say her name and cause the whole world to vanish, is the same man who almost killed her brother.

Because this man, whose left hand glints with the gold of her future, and whose shaking fingers lift and hold out her own ring that will secure her once again as his and his and his, is the same man who almost killed her brother.

Delia closes her eyes, and tries to replace the image of Ben's face with that of her brother's, but Ben just does not fade. In fact, with her eyes closed, she can see him even more clearly. This whole tragedy has proven to her now, beyond any doubt, that Ben Starre is her destiny. Surely, if anything was going to lessen her feelings for him, it would be the knowledge that he tried to kill someone she loves. Yet, here she is, drawn to him still. So now, raw in the absolute naked truth that nothing could ever diminish their love, she opens her eyes, and she opens her hand, and as he slips the wedding ring back on her finger, she opens up her whole world to him.

Ben touches her face. He tucks a strand of hair behind her ear. And then he slowly presses his lips hot against her brow, stifling his own sob with her skin as she absorbs his apology.

Delia grazes his jawbone with her teeth, marking him with the Morse code of forgiveness.

Above them, stars light, one by one, like candle flames, and the darkening sky billows over them like a blanket. They sink into the bed of each other's bodies where nothing else exists except the fierce and true power of devotion, which will surely burn away everything that has gone wrong today, and leave behind in its glowing wake all that is right.

Weaving through the garden, as silent as the shadows

that cloak them, they slip into the empty house. In her room, Delia watches as Ben's eyes take in her two large suitcases, and the pink envelope on her pillow.

He turns to her, his face glowing with hope, and reaches out to cup her cheek.

She nods her certainty into it, and as his eyes brighten with tears, his fingers curl into a fist, trapping within his palm this acknowledgment that their bond is unbroken and unbreakable.

When Ben's lips part, perhaps to let out his apology, his regret, his appreciation, Delia comes up on her toes to seal his mouth with her own silent understanding.

Then she breaks away from him, stoops and grabs the handle of one suitcase.

He smiles and takes the other.

And then they hear footsteps on the stairs.

Light steps. Quick. Birdlike.

Ben spins and grabs both bags and shuts the wardrobe door silently behind him, just as the handle of the bedroom door squeaks as it turns.

Imogen Rose's large blue eyes are red rimmed and puffy and she looks as if she has been shattered and glued back together. Tiny black cracks and holes can be seen if you know where to look for the fault lines. And Delia certainly does know. Because she made some of those in the past. And she is about to make more of them now.

'Hello, my darling girl,' Imogen says, as she sits on the edge of the bed. 'I'm so glad you are here.'

Her voice is serrated, and the edges of it slice ragged gashes through Delia's resolve.

She prays her mother has been made stronger by the past, strong enough to withstand the blow that is to come. Thinking of Ben crouched in the wardrobe with her suitcases and goodbye letter, thinking of Claude unconscious in the hospital, Delia wonders if her mother is on the verge of losing just one of her children, or both, and then with a jolt Delia wonders why her mother is suddenly here, in her room, looking so very broken.

Delia sinks onto the bed too. 'What's wrong? Claude?'

'Is the same.' Imogen smiles, and her face is instantly warm. 'The hospital is just running some more tests, so your father and I came home to get some of his things, you know, so he'll feel at home once he wakes up. No, Claude isn't the reason I need to talk to you.'

Imogen reaches out a fluttering hand and Delia takes it and holds it and tries to commit its bony feel to memory, unsure of when she will get to do this again.

'Your father and I have been talking,' Imogen says. 'We know how worried you are about Claude, but he is stable and, really, there's not much you can do here except worry. We think it will do you good to have a little distraction.' She smiles. 'He's organised for you and Guy Shylock to go away for a couple of days. Maybe get to know each other better.'

'What?' Delia shakes her head. 'Why?'

'Because he's perfect for you, dear. Your father and I can see that, even if you can't.' She leans forward and smiles. 'I saw that kiss you shared at the party.'

'No, he's *not* perfect for me at all! This is ridiculous. I'm not going!'

There is a soft tap on the door and her father pushes it open. Haloed by the light of the hallway, and with his white skin and white hair glowing, Shepherd Rose looms as large as God. 'Did you tell her the good news, Imogen?'

'Daddy,' Delia stands and places a hand on his arm. 'I appreciate what you're trying to do, but I'm not going away with Guy.'

'Why not? You should be proud that someone like *Guy* is interested in you.'

She flinches as his words strike her. 'I don't need you to find me a husband.'

'You listen to me!' he shouts.

His voice crashes against the walls of Delia's bedroom, and she falls back onto the bed, stunned at the force that rolls from him like a tide. Her father has never raised his voice to her in all her life, and its reverberation leaves her shivering.

'You *will* go with Guy tomorrow morning if I have to physically drag you there myself! And once you're there, you will enjoy Guy's company! Understood?'

'Darling ...' Imogen places an unsteady hand on her husband's arm. 'It's not *that* big a deal. If she doesn't want to go, she doesn't have to.'

But, for the first time in Delia's life, her father acts as if her mother doesn't even exist. His voice lowers to a whisper that is far more frightening somehow than his shouts had been. 'You will go away with Guy, or you will no longer be welcome in this house.'

'Well, that's perfectly fine with me!' Delia says, shooting to her feet.

'What? No!' Her mother yells, gripping onto Delia's hand again. 'Shepherd Rose, how dare you speak to our daughter like that!'

'*Our* daughter?' He rounds on her.

She shrinks away.

'She's no daughter of mine. If she is not willing to do this *one* thing for me, after I raised her and provided for her!' His whole face changes then, as if something inside gives way. He collapses in on himself like an imploding building crashing down, floor by floor. He takes a shaky breath and fixes suddenly frightened eyes on Delia. 'We'll lose everything.' His voice is thin. Pleading. 'We're broke.'

'What?' Imogen gapes at him. 'What do you mean?'

'I mean, we're broke,' he says again, still looking right at Delia. 'The bank is taking the business, the house, the land, everything. In three days.'

'How can we be broke?' whispers Imogen.

'Three days,' he says. 'Unless I can get the money together. And Guy has agreed to give it to us, on the condition that you go away with him.' Shepherd steps forward and takes Delia's hand. 'Please, Delia, I don't want to put this all on you, but you are my only option now. You can save us. Save *me*. Our financial future is in your hands. You don't have to go, it is your decision. I only hope you make the right one.'

A single tear traces his cheek as he turns, avoids Imogen's shocked gaze, and hurries from the room with his shoulders rounded by shame.

'Shepherd Rose, do not walk away from me!' calls Imogen, as she slams the bedroom door closed behind her.

Delia has never seen her father cry before. The image rocks her to the core.

We're broke? she thinks, turning the word, and all its derivatives, around in her mind. Broke. Broken. To break. How ironic that it's all up to her to keep this family from breaking apart, when all she wants to do is leave them and break it apart.

Shaking, Delia opens the wardrobe door and blinks down at the one person who has the power to hold her together. Ben slumps against the wall, his face is as pale as a corpse, and for a heart-stopping moment Delia can see him, as if dead, as if in the bottom of a tomb. She has a feeling that if she does not leave with him tonight, that she will not see him alive again.

'You heard all that?' she asks.

'Hard not to.' He stands, and is once again full of so much life that is swells into her. 'You have to stay here.'

'No!' She shakes her head. 'I told you that if we are

married, then I will follow you to the ends of the earth. I meant it.'

He shushes her with a kiss and right then she knows she will do whatever he says because she simply doesn't have the strength to oppose him.

'Hear me out,' he says. 'Just stay here for a few days. A week, maybe. Go away with that jerk, get your father the money he needs, then you can slip away and meet up with me, and we'll just disappear.'

'But I want to be with you, *now*, today, tomorrow ...'

'And you *can* be,' he says. 'But you have to do this for your family first. Please, after everything they are going through ...'

He doesn't say the words, 'because of me', but she hears them all the same.

'Why?' she says, fisting her hands. 'Why should I help *him* after what he just said to me? He's practically *selling* me!'

'Because, he's your *father*,' says Ben, simply. 'And because it's the right thing to do.'

'But ...'

'And,' he says, closing his eyes, 'because I need you to.'

Delia sighs. There it is. Her decision made.

'Just give me a kiss and let me go. We'll be together soon.'

So Delia lifts herself up to him, rising like grief, and pours as much of herself into him as she can. Then, without a word – because, really, what words could possibly exist in the vacuum of this moment – Ben opens the bedroom window, climbs out onto the drainpipe and slides to the ground, where he disappears into the dark and the shadows like a ghost.

chapter twenty-one

Out of the dark and the shadows of Puck's front porch, Guy Shylock's white toothy grin comes forward.

'Guy!' Puck steps back to let his old college roommate cross the threshold. 'How are you, bud?'

'I'm good.' Guy grins even wider. 'No, I'm *great*, actually!'

'Well, that's the best way to be,' Puck says and leads Guy down the hall into the lounge, where a smouldering joint waits.

Guy tips his head to the side and smiles at the blue lava lamp blobbing away on top of the television, and the TV screen projecting nothing but snow.

'Good to see you learnt something in school.'

Puck smiles and sits and offers Guy the joint. 'I'm just winding down for the evening. Care to join me?'

'You know I can't say no to that.' Guy takes the cigarette between his fingers.

They sit in silence for a beat, letting the smoke cloud

them in its warm fuzziness, and watching the white flurry of dots on the TV screen morph into the image of two doves in flight, a speeding car, a beating heart.

'So,' Puck says, 'what's been happening?'

'Oh, man,' Guy shakes his head, 'I've gone and got myself totally hung up on a chick. I mean *totally* hung up! I can't sleep, I can't eat; you know, all the old clichés that I never thought were true.'

'Sure sounds like love! Congratulations,' says Puck, and then he mutters, 'Must be something in the water lately.'

'You know; I think it *is* love. I think it really is! Only, now, I need to convince *her* of that.'

Christ, what is going on with the guys in this town all falling in love, or at least lust, with women that simply are not interested? First Ben gets hung up on Olivia, but at least he's sorted out now, thanks to Delia Rose. And now Guy is here, getting all woozy over someone who obviously is not all woozy for him.

Puck sighs. 'Anything I can do to help?'

'Actually,' Guy says, handing back the joint, 'that's why I'm here. See, I'm taking her away tomorrow for a few days. But it has to be somewhere special. So, I was wondering, man, if you still have that house where we used to party during the summer?'

Thinking about the keys to his beach house, which are right this minute tucked safely away in Ben Starre's pocket, Puck splutters on his mouthful of smoke. 'Yeah, man, I do,' he says, recovering. 'But I've got someone staying in it at the moment. Sorry, bud.'

'Oh really? Bummer.' Guy shrugs. 'Well, maybe I'll take her to the town anyway; it's beautiful and it has some gorgeous hotels right on the beach.'

'Yeah, good idea, sorry I couldn't hook you up. So, who's the lucky girl, anyway?'

Guy pauses, and his chest expands, as if allowing the chick's name to fill him up before breathing it out in a whisper. 'Delia Rose.'

Puck chokes again, hunching over and coughing until his eyes stream with tears.

'You know Delia, right?' Guy asks. 'She's Shepherd Rose's daughter.'

'Oh, yeah,' Puck says, wiping his watering eyes. 'I know her.'

'She's great, isn't she?' Guy seems to expand even more. 'She's so beautiful, and smart, and graceful. Man, I must have accrued some bloody good karma in a past life to get someone like her to go with me, hey?'

'Wait.' Puck sits up straighter. 'You mean, she's *agreed* to go away with you?'

'Her father just called and told me she would, so yeah. I mean, it'll be good for her to get away, get her mind on *other* things,' he winks, 'you know, besides her brother's accident. You heard about that?'

'Oh, yes, I heard about that all right.'

There's a sudden knock on the door like the ticking

of a clock – *tap tap tap* – and Guy springs to his feet and shakes Puck's hand. 'Well, I'd better get going. Got a lot to organise. We should catch up soon, okay? It's been far too long. When I get back, I'll bring around a few beers, it'll be like old times.'

'Sure,' Puck says, wondering why he is so popular tonight, as he follows his friend down the hall.

Guy opens the front door to let himself out and then jumps backwards, stepping on Puck's toes.

'Ouch! What the ...' Puck leans around Guy to see who is at his door this time, and he has to fight the urge not to laugh. This night is just getting ridiculous now.

Delia Rose blinks up from the threshold.

Guy's smile fades as he looks at her face, which is so obviously sad. He lifts a hand, as if to reach out, to hold her, but then he drops it back to his side. 'Hi,' he whispers.

She lifts her chin, and her eyes narrow and she stares at him. 'I didn't realise *you* would be here.'

'What a lovely surprise, then,' he says.

She rolls her eyes, and pushes by him into the hallway.

'I can't wait for tomorrow,' he calls after her. 'You're going to have a great time, I promise.'

And Puck hears her muttered response, 'We'll see.'

Puck looks at his old friend, who stands once again on the doorstep, but now that illuminating grin is gone, and he seems completely deflated.

Guy shrugs a shoulder and tries to cough out a laugh.

'Don't let her go boring you with how much she loves me!'

Puck tries to smile back, but can feel it turning into a grimace of pity.

'Put in a good word for me?' Guy asks, before letting out a great sigh, nodding a goodbye, and pulling the door closed.

Back in the lounge room, Delia paces back and forth across the rug. 'Can you *believe* that guy?'

'He told me you two are going away for a few days.' Puck leans against the doorframe and watches her. 'He's quite excited.'

'He should be; he's paying enough for it! Oh, he didn't mention that? What a surprise! Apparently, my father's in debt, and Guy's promised to give him the money he needs on the condition that I go away with him! He's buying my companionship, and now he expects me to swoon at his feet in love?'

'No, Delia, you've got him all wrong. Guy Shylock is one of the most caring people I know.'

She huffs. 'Are we talking about the same guy?'

'I was with him in the city this one night; it was winter, freezing cold. Anyway, we see this drunken old bum passed out on a bench, reeking of cheap whisky. Guy took off this brand new coat he'd bought just that afternoon – not a cheap coat either, let me add – drapes it over this dude, and keeps walking as if nothing out of the ordinary happened. When I asked him why he gave the man his coat, he shrugged, as if the question had never occurred to him, and then said through his chattering teeth: "He looked like he needed a coat."'

She stops pacing and crosses her arms. 'What's your point?'

'My point is,' says Puck, 'that I know Guy; we were roommates for three years. I'd bet my life that he would give your father that money whether you were going away with him or not.'

'Really?'

'Really,' he says gently.

'Then why is he making me whore myself?'

'It's not like that. He *likes* you, Delia. And in case you didn't notice, he turns into a bit of a nervous idiot around girls he likes. He always has. He just wants a chance to show you the real him.'

'Well, I don't want to see the real Guy. In case you have forgotten, Puck, I'm *married* to Ben! Remember? I can't go gallivanting across the country on romantic trips with other men – nice as they may be. Christ, how the hell am I supposed to get out of this?'

'Maybe,' Puck says, smiling as an idea becomes clear in his cloudy brain, 'you *don't* get out of it.'

She whirls on him. 'Do you think this is some kind of joke? Played out especially for your amusement?'

'Listen.' Puck holds up his hands. 'I spoke to Ben earlier. He has gone away to stay in my holiday home across the state line. It's a beautiful secluded property right on the beach; double storey with a balcony where you can sit and watch the waves all day.'

'What does this have to do with anything?'

'Guy came here tonight to ask me if *he* could use that house for a few days. He is planning on taking you to the very same town, Delia. And once you are there, just explain the whole story.'

She frowns at him. 'Are you insane?'

'Like I said, he's a good guy. He'll understand. I bet he'll even be happy for the two of you, even at the expense of his own happiness. Your father will be out of debt, and you will be free to stay with Ben. This couldn't have worked out better, really.'

'I can think of a few ways it could have worked out better,' she mutters. 'But, you really think this could work?'

Puck lifts the joint to his lips. 'What could go wrong?'

'Famous last words.' She rolls her eyes, but they are no longer dull and angry. Her sparkle is back.

'Here.' Puck offers her the joint, but she shakes her head.

'No.' She sighs and rubs her eyes with the heels of her hands, 'Although, it might help me sleep.'

'Trouble sleeping?'

'I haven't slept one wink; I was awake all last night, first with Ben at the party, and then thinking about him afterwards, and now, although I'm exhausted, there are so many thoughts going through me there's no way I'll sleep tonight, not with everything that is happening: Claude's accident, Ben's leaving, Dad's debt, Guy's invitation, and now this promise of being with Ben again by tomorrow! God, I just wish I could shut off my brain for a while, you know? Escape my thoughts with a sleep so deep that not even dreams can reach me.'

'Well,' Puck looks down at the tin on the coffee table. 'I have some sleeping pills if you want some?'

'No.' She shakes her head. 'I don't know. I've never been a big fan of them.'

Flipping up the lid of the tin, he pulls out a small plastic bottle. 'Take one of these; even if you have the strength of twenty men, it will knock you out cold! You'll sleep like the dead and then awake as if from a pleasant sleep.'

'Well,' she shrugs and smiles and takes the bottle from Puck's hand, 'what can go wrong?'

chapter twenty-two

The lights are out and the house is dark when Delia pulls into the drive, which suits her just fine, thank you very much. She doesn't want to run into that traitor of a father. She can't believe he is doing this; she's not a piece of meat, not a possession that he has the right to sell off.

She belongs to no one.

Not even Ben Starre.

Yes, he has her heart, and yes, he has her hand, but she is still herself, and no one but she can ever own that.

In her room, she lies on her bed and stares up at the ceiling.

How could he do this to her? Her own father.

And then Katherine, who's supposed to be her best friend no matter what. Who is supposed to have Delia's back no matter what. Who is supposed to agree with her no matter what.

But no.

Two of the most important people in her life, on

whom she thought she could always rely, have betrayed her tonight.

Delia replays their conversation in her head, balling her fists in anger just as fiercely as she had when she'd been on the phone.

'Oh, Katherine,' she'd sobbed, once she heard her friend's comforting voice on the other end of the line. Delia told her about Guy, and her father's nasty ultimatum, and that Ben had told her to agree to everything before slipping out her window and vanishing.

'Wow,' breathed Katherine, after a moment's silence.

'Yeah. Wow.' Delia agreed. 'So what should I do? I don't want to go away with Guy; he's such a sleaze. Help me.'

'You know what,' said Katherine, 'I think you should do it, too. At least give Guy a proper chance, he's probably not that bad. I think he's sweet. I think he'd treat you right. And remember that kiss you shared at the party? That looked pretty intense from where I'd been standing.'

'What?' Delia shook her head. 'What do you mean?'

'I mean,' she sighed heavily through the phone, 'I think you should forget about Ben and go for Guy.'

'Ben is my husband!' Delia stammered. 'And you're supposed to be my friend; how can you even think that?'

'Exactly, I'm your friend, which means I have your best interests at heart. Ben obviously has a short fuse

– take today as the perfect example. You don't want someone like that in the long run. And Guy is nice; okay, he's a little boastful, but he is a nice guy.'

'I thought *you* wanted Guy?' she snapped.

'Nah, I think he's too soft for me. But I could see you being truly happy with him. And also,' Katherine paused, 'Juliet was forced to marry Paris and she refused, and ended up dead. Guy is your Paris.'

'Oh, so that's what this is about! That Shakespeare stuff again?'

'I know you think I'm crazy, but I really believe there's something in this. You have to choose a different path than Juliet did. Marry Paris. I mean Guy.'

'For the last time, I am *not* Juliet!'

'Hey, I'm just saying what I think – you asked.'

'Fine,' Delia sighed. 'You know what? You're right. Thanks Katherine, you're a good friend. What would I do without you?'

'So, you're going to give Guy a shot?' Katherine asked.

'Looks that way, doesn't it?'

'Good for you,' said Katherine. 'You're doing the right thing.'

And so, Delia had said goodnight and hung up before Katherine heard the truth beneath the lies. Delia had never felt so alone in her life: her best friend betrayed her, her husband was on the run, her brother was in hospital, and her father was selling her happiness for a bunch of grapes.

So, Delia had grabbed her keys and headed to the only person left in whom she could confide.

Now, Delia reaches for the bottle of pills from Puck and unscrews the lid. They roll into her palm like tiny promises of numbing bliss.

And she almost drops them when a soft knock taps on her door.

'Delia?' Imogen whispers from the hall.

Fumbling to get the pills back in the bottle, Delia replaces the lid and shoves the bottle under her pillow. 'Come in.'

Imogen opens the door and smiles into the room. 'Are you all right? I'm so sorry about earlier. I've never seen your father lose his temper like that. Well, not since ...' She shakes her head. 'It must have been such a strain on him to keep a giant secret for so long.'

'It's okay, I understand. In fact, I agree with him. I've decided to go away with Guy.'

'Well, that's nice, sweetheart. But I came in here to tell you, you don't have to go just because of what that great lug said earlier; he didn't *mean* it. If you don't want to go, then you don't have to. Leave your father up to me, I'll sort him out.'

'Thank you,' Delia says. 'But, no, I really *do* want to go.' A cold finger of fear crackles up her spine and almost freezes up the heat of her life; she is about to run away, to leave her brother in a critical state, to leave her father stressed about money, to leave her mother who is prepared to stand up for her no matter what. This woman is prepared to risk her home, her business, her livelihood, all for Delia's happiness.

Tears well and tickle down Delia's cheeks, and she reaches out a hand. 'Mummy,' she whispers, and suddenly words spill from Delia even faster than her tears. All her words, all her truths rush out like a tide.

Imogen's eyes widen and grow wider still with every revelation. 'Ben Starre?' She whispers, and lifts Delia's left hand, staring at the ring that glints on the third finger. Her cheeks pale and she shakes her head. 'No! No, you can't have.'

'We met,' says Delia, 'we fell in love, we exchanged vows.'

'Oh my God.' Imogen's hand flutters over the black hole of her mouth.

'I'm sorry we didn't tell you, but we didn't think you'd approve, and it was the only way we could get around Burgundy's rules and be able to legally see each other. And besides,' she smiles and takes Imogen's hand, 'we really *do* love each other. It was instant. The connection we felt, it was just like you and Daddy, right down to the electric spark you always talk about. Well, we had that too! Love at first sight, Mum. We'll be just as perfect as you and Daddy have always been.'

Still shaking her head, Imogen reaches out and presses Delia's hand between both of hers. 'Sweetheart, you should go away with Guy tomorrow. Forget about Ben!'

'But ... you just said I *shouldn't* go if I don't want to.'

'Well, it's for the best. Trust me.'

'Ben really *is* a beautiful soul, Mum. What happened with Claude today was just an accident. I know you have some kind of beef with the Mr and Mrs Starre, and you've kept us separated all these years, but I know that if you and Dad just give him a chance, you'll see why I fell for Ben so quickly and so hard.'

'Oh, Delia,' she swallows and tears glisten in her eyes. 'I always hoped this day would never come. Your father always said it would, always threatened that the truth needed to come out, but I thought we could all just keep going along as we are.'

'What are you talking about?'

Imogen closes her eyes. 'It's time you learned the reason that our family has been fighting with the Starres for so many years.'

chapter twenty-three

Claude's sleepy weight was heavy and lovely in Imogen's arms as she lifted him from his car seat. He clenched his chubby fists in her hair and snuggled his face into her neck. She inhaled his scent of baby shampoo, and felt that wonderful warm flutter of *motheriness* as she walked up the path to the front door.

The wind was cold and it ruffled Claude's downy hair with icy fingers. As Imogen turned away from it, trying as best she could to shield her son, she was struck by a recurring and terrible thought: she would be unable to protect her baby from the dangers of this world. As he grows, the world will rear up around him, and his innocence will surely be a tempting challenge, something that fate will want to take for herself, and there is nothing, absolutely nothing, that Imogen can ever do to stop it.

She shivered as she hurried up the path, held Claude closer to her chest, and rang the doorbell, waiting for the smiling face of her best friend to appear and usher them into the warm safety of this home.

But, it was not Desdemona who opened the door.

'Morgan?' Imogen said and smiled nervously at him. 'I didn't expect you to be here.'

'Sorry to disappoint,' he said.

'Oh, no, I didn't mean …'

He smiled then and stepped back to allow her and Claude to enter. 'It's fine, Imogen. Come in. Mona has just popped out to the grocery store. She said she'd only be a few minutes, which unfortunately means that you'll have to put up with me for about an hour or two!'

As Imogen slipped past him into the foyer, Morgan leaned forward and made a face at Claude. 'My, he is growing fast, isn't he?'

'Too fast,' Imogen agreed. 'It actually scares me a little. But you'll know all about it yourself soon.' She grinned at him. 'Right?'

Morgan's face changed in an instant. Where there had been light and laughter and joy suddenly darkened into a storm cloud that swirled black behind his eyes. 'She told you, did she?'

'Uh …' Imogen stammered, unsure exactly what she'd said to upset him. 'Mona told me that you two are trying for a baby. She said you were both very excited about it.'

He grunted and turned away, heading for the living room. 'You can wait in here, if you like. Help yourself to coffee or juice or whatever. I'll be in my den.'

'Wait, Morgan!' she called after him.

He stopped, but didn't turn to face her.

'If I've said something to offend you,' said Imogen, 'I'm sorry. I didn't mean anything.'

'She told you we were trying for a baby,' he said. 'But did she tell you that it's pointless, that we can't have one, and it's all my fault?'

'What?' Her mouth dropped open. 'Oh, Morgan ...'

Finally, he turned, and his face was completely disfigured by grief.

Imogen settled the sleeping Claude onto the sofa, and she stepped towards Morgan.

What was she supposed to do? Did she hug him? Did she place a gentle hand on his forearm? Did she simply stand there and offer the comfort of her silent presence?

He stared down at the sleeping baby curled up on his couch cushions. Claude pouted in his sleep, and he fisted his chubby fingers, and as Morgan Starre watched this infant sleep, he let tears fall free down his cheeks. He didn't even try to wipe them away.

'People in this town think I am a successful man. I have a beautiful wife. A booming business. A fat bank account. But no amount of money in the world can buy you a higher sperm count. Sure it can buy fertility drugs but so far they haven't done anything! All I ever wanted to be,' he whispered, 'was a father. So really, despite everything I have, I'm just a big failure.'

'Oh, that's not true!' Imogen said.

But he looked at her then, and she realised she had absolutely no words that could back up her claim. She looked down at Claude, and was overwhelmed by her love for him; the thought of not having this child in her life left her breathless.

So, urged forward by the sudden need to ease this man's pain, Imogen wrapped her arms around him, and held him close.

He stiffened and Imogen thought he was going to push her away.

But then, slowly, his arms came around her. His heart throbbed like a solid force against her chest. His breath blew hot against her ear. She closed her eyes and tried to remember the last time she felt the heat of another adult pressing this close to her.

Shepherd had barely even looked in her direction for weeks.

She couldn't remember the last time Shepherd had touched her.

And she had also forgotten how nice it could be.

When Morgan kissed her on the cheek, it was friendly. When he kissed her on the forehead, it was grateful. And by the time he leaned down and finally pressed his lips on hers, it was hesitant and then hungry and then desperate.

Or maybe that was just how *she* felt.

Because now she remembered what it was like to be wanted by another person, and if she closed her eyes, she could almost pretend that person was her husband. Almost. But not quite. Because Morgan smelled different. And felt different. And moved different.

But what was not different was the *need*. The need to be wanted. And the need to want.

After they made love – right there on the lounge room floor with Imogen's sleeping child only feet away – they scurried to dress, they mumbled apologies to each other, and they did not meet the other's gaze for fear they would each see within the ugly and sneering face of shame.

Neither of them could ever take back what had just happened. They could not go back in time and unbetray the two people that they loved. So maybe they could simply go forward and pretend that it had never happened.

Because, after all, if they didn't tell, how on earth would anyone ever find out?

chapter twenty-four

Delia stares at her mother, who stops speaking and won't make eye contact. 'Mum,' she whispers, 'please don't tell me what I think you're going to tell me.'

'I'm sorry!' Imogen sobs. 'I'm so, *so* sorry, but it just … happened.'

The earlier words of Shepherd Rose suddenly shout at Delia again in her memory: '*Our daughter? She's no daughter of mine! After I raised her and provided for her …*'

'Are you telling me,' she gasps, 'that you had an affair? That you cheated on Daddy? That Morgan Starre,' she bites her lip, barely believing these words are coming out of her mouth, 'Morgan Starre is my *father*?'

Imogen hesitates, and in that second Delia feels hope rise warm and safe around her shoulders like a woollen shawl. All she has to do is laugh, and say, *No, don't be silly, I would never do that to your father, you know how we are, you've seen how much we love each other, and the way we have always looked at each other as if falling in love all over again with each glance.*

But Imogen doesn't say that.

She just nods.

And everything just unravels.

'Yes,' Imogen whispers. 'It's true. It's all true. Your father and I learned how to act like nothing happened in the hopes that maybe we could forget that it ever did. But the thing about acting is that you are always playing a character. I am his wife, and he is my husband, but for years they have been nothing but our roles. And we became very good at portraying them.'

Delia's face screws up with effort and pain as she speaks the next sentence, every word embedding into her heart like a shard of glass. 'And so, all these years, he was just portraying the role of my father?'

'I'm so sorry, baby,' Imogen says.

'And ...' Delia closes her eyes and with a Herculean effort forces out the next words, which have her gasping from the sharp sting as they sink deep into her heart. 'And Ben?'

'Ben Starre,' Imogen says, still not looking at her, 'is your half-brother.'

Delia does not remember her mother leaving the room.

She doesn't know how long she has rocked, how long she has stared, how long she has cried, how long she has muttered the words, 'half-brother' over and over like a God damn crazy person in a psych ward.

Oh, God, no, this is not right; this is not how her life is meant to play out! After all these patient and frustrating years, her soul mate has finally, *finally*, come along, only to be revealed, not as her true love, but as her *brother*! She wishes she could call Katherine and tell her this, because Delia is sure as sugar that *this* incestuous twist never befell the likes of Romeo and God damn Juliet.

God, that stupid play.

And those two stupid characters.

And how lucky they both were!

The love between Juliet and her Romeo lives on and on and on, forever, as a benchmark to all other loves. And yet, this love? The love between Delia and Ben? Well, that love is dirty, and something no sane person would ever hope to feel.

And yet, its intensity is in no way dulled by this new truth.

At least, not for Delia.

And what kind of person does that make her?

Is she sick? Deranged? Perverted?

When she imagines Ben's face, and the feel of his lips on hers, and his breath in her lungs, and his heat pulsing within her, she shivers with delight and she craves more.

Yet, she knows she can never be with him again.

Can she?

How will he react when he learns that she is his sister?

Will he be revolted by the intimacy they have shared?

She starts to sob again.

If he is disgusted, then she has no choice but to love him from afar for the rest of her life, pretending to all the world that the love she feels for him is merely kinship. She can do this easily. Hell, she's grown up watching the two best actors in world pretend to be in love; surely she can pretend *not* to be.

They can both move on with their lives, they can be married, and have children, and grow old with other people who surely will not instil within them the same burning desire that they felt for each other.

If he *is* disgusted, she will not have to fight this internal struggle with herself.

If he *is* disgusted, then he will not want her.

But, what if his love, like hers, is untarnished by this new revelation, and they will then have to decide which path to choose: what *feels* right, or what *is* right?

As much as they love each other, they could never come together to create a family whose DNA is the same on both sides.

Unless ...

Unless the truth never comes out?

She could continue on with her plan, unperturbed. She could go away with Guy tomorrow, and leave him for Ben, and they could run away and live their lives and not return, and Ben would never have to know. They will both be leaving their families behind. She could protect him from it all. She could save him from the torment that will now plague her forever. She could ensure that at least one of their hearts remains pure in love.

She could live in sin and dishonesty with a man whose heart contains blood the same as her own.

Oh God, oh God, oh God.

Rolling over, Delia moves slowly through the fog that surrounds her. Her arms are heavy as if the air itself has been thickened with the horror of her new situation. And as her hand searches beneath the pillow for the small, white bottle of pills, she thinks again of me, and my prediction.

An age-old spite will once again be rife among those who've branched from the first quarrel. The streets will flow with crimson's tide of life, and stain the hands, and minds, of those moral. From each side of this battlefield romance will bloom between you and one forbidden. Your love will break the spell of hatred's trance, and uncover a secret long-hidden. Bitterness dissolved and old wounds healed, this peace comes at a grave and mortal price: two deaths. This noble bargain will be sealed, hatred buried by love's self-sacrifice. Love conquers all; a proverb that's on cue, for you may prove this old adage is true.

A hollow laugh escapes her.

Love conquers all? How can love conquer all in this situation? Love is dead, it is not conquering anything, except maybe her will to live.

Ben is her brother.

Her life's love – her husband – is her brother.

Love conquers all? Delia thinks, unscrewing the bottle cap. Not in my story.

She can't take this any longer. These thoughts. These questions. This torment. She wants peace. Beautiful, empty, silent peace. At least until morning.

At her dressing table, she reaches for a half-empty glass of water, and freezes as she stares at her reflection.

Christ, how could her mother have done this to her? Her beautiful mother with her white-blonde hair, and eyes like blue diamonds.

Delia had started bleaching her hair as soon as she was old enough; she was the only one in her family that had dark hair, and she'd told herself she was doing it because it was cool and that is what all the cool girls were doing. But what if, subconsciously, she had known the truth of her heritage all along, and had just wanted to look more like a blond Rose, like her mother, instead of a brunette Starre.

And her eyes, her *dark brown* eyes. God, she was an idiot. She'd passed high school biology. Brown eyes from two blue-eyed parents? Brown eyes, that were so blind to the truth, stared right out at her every day from the mirror. It was so obvious.

She closes her eyes but the cessation of sight does nothing to stop the vision of thought and the pain that is pulled along behind, like a child trailing a balloon.

A single pill rattles from the bottle and lands silently in the meat of her palm. It sounds like a promise and she fists her hand over it, making a silent wish as she lifts her arm and shoots the pill into her mouth, washing it down with the stale water.

Then she lays back on her bed and waits for the silence to enfold her like an ocean.

But nothing happens. She stares at the ceiling and batts away at the thoughts that will not leave her alone. Until she reaches for the bottle a second time, and then after another brief period of hell, she reaches for it again.

As she swallows the third pill, her mind becomes suddenly woollen, as though wrapped in a thick blanket, and wonders if she has been too impatient. Her eyes are too heavy to keep open, and she lets the world go black as she remembers Puck's words from earlier that day: *Take one of these; even if you have the strength of twenty men, it will knock you out cold! You'll sleep like the dead and then awake as if from a pleasant sleep.*

Take one, he had said. One.

Has she taken too many now?

Or, has she not taken enough?

What if she takes another one?

Another two?

The rest of the bottle?

To live, or not to live? That is the question.

Maybe that is also the answer to all of this.

Would it be so bad if she didn't wake up? A gift of peace to the one she loves. Does she want to live without his love anyway?

And Ben, when he hears the news – both of her death and of their shared parentage – he can forget her and move on with his life. Maybe with that girl whose name she'd seen tattooed on his arm. *Olivia*. The tattoo is fresh, still healing. Perhaps this Olivia's love would have the power to heal the wounds on his heart as easily as on his skin.

Delia imagines her body found here in the morning. By whom? Her father? Her mother? She sees it zipped up inside a thick black body bag. She sees it naked and waiting inside the cold sterile draw in the morgue.

With cement arms she reaches for the phone. But as her sleeve drops, she focuses blurrily on her left wrist, on the raised white scar there.

She promised her mother she wouldn't again. Not again. She promised her.

But then, Imogen Rose wasn't exactly the best keeper of promises, now was she?

Maybe there is no such thing as fate? Maybe the stars do not control the decisions we make, and they do not set out our destiny? Maybe, in the end, we choose our own path despite what fate has planned?

Maybe she took too many pills. Maybe she took just enough.

Letting fate guide her now, Delia snuggles down under her blankets and smiles as images of Ben come and take her away.

chapter twenty-five

Imogen halts on the landing and presses her ear against her daughter's bedroom door. Raising her fingers to knock, she pauses.

Maybe she should just let Delia sleep? She needs her rest after all.

It was past midnight before she heard Delia's sobs quieten and go as silent as the dead.

Instead of knocking, she flattens her palm against the wood and then lets her fist fall to her side. The real reason she doesn't want to wake her daughter is not because she's a caring, generous mother who wants the best for her daughter, it is because she's a selfish and gutless excuse for a mother and a wife. It is because her daughter, who used to gaze up at her with awe, will look up at her this morning the way she did last night. The way Shep always looks at her. Even though he doesn't mean to. Even though he probably doesn't even know he is doing it. That look is always there. Always. Beneath every smile.

Beneath every kind word. Beneath every forced: 'I love you'.

Imogen lost her husband. She may be about to lose her son. She doesn't want to look in her daughter's face and see proof that she has lost Delia, too. Even if it is what she deserves.

Sniffing back tears, Imogen walks away from Delia's door just as the front doorbell rings.

Katherine smiles at Imogen from the porch. 'Good morning, Mrs R. Is Delia up yet? She's not answering my calls or texts. She's totally pissed at me.'

She's totally pissed at me too, Imogen thinks. With a pang, she realises that, in as little as a few minutes, Delia will confide her secret to her best friend, and Imogen's life as she knows it will end.

And surprisingly, she is relieved. After all these years of living a lie, how freeing will it be to shrug off those heavy robes and be herself again?

'She's still sleeping,' Imogen says to Katherine. 'She had a bit of a rough night last night.'

'I'll go wake her.' Katherine slips up the stairs before Imogen can stop her.

She wonders how fast the word will spread through the town. How long before everybody is talking about it. About them. About poor Desdemona Starre and the way her best friend and husband betrayed her.

Imogen's eyes burn with the guilt she's carried for so many years, but she blinks away the tears.

Even though she and Desdemona Starre are no longer friends, Imogen does not want this old wound reopened for her. She still can't believe that she actually did that to her friend. All Desdemona had wanted was a baby, a baby that was going to be difficult to conceive due to her husband's low sperm count, and Imogen had just waltzed in one day, and stolen one of those precious little sperms for herself, and conceived the child that should have been Desdemona's. Sure, Morgan had gone on to father two more children, Ben and Orlando, but still, that wasn't really the point, was it?

Imogen winces as a shrill scream peals from Delia's bedroom.

Well, thinks Imogen, here we go. Katherine knows. And soon, so will everyone else.

But when the scream comes again, Imogen recognises it as not one of anger, or one of shock, but one of *fear*, and one that is calling out her name.

'Mrs Rose! Help! Help me!'

She doesn't remember running up the stairs. She simply blinks and is standing in the bedroom doorway, frowning down in confusion. Delia is in bed. Still dressed in the clothes she'd worn the day before. Shoelaces still neatly tied. A pool of dried silvery vomit on the pillow.

Imogen breathes her daughter's name, and then she screams it, and then she crawls onto the bed and shakes Delia, who flops like a rag doll, and a white bottle of pills drops from somewhere, and her lips are blue, and her skin is white, and Imogen places an ear against Delia's mouth but there is no hot breeze of breath, and she knows that her daughter is dead, and she knows that this is all her fault.

chapter twenty-six

This is all my fault, thinks Guy Shylock, as he steps towards the hospital bed, in which Delia Rose lies fragile as a broken vase. Her chest rises and falls in rhythm with the machine that breathes for her, and Guy wonders if her heart needs support to keep going, because he would surely give his own heart; it beats for her every second, anyway.

He knew Delia hadn't wanted to go away with him. But he also knew that they had shared something pretty special the other night on the dance floor. He had not imagined the force of that kiss. He knew she had felt it, too. Hadn't she?

He shouldn't have pressured her into going away with him. He shouldn't have pressured her father into making it happen. God, what an awful thing to do! He'd taken advantage of Shepherd's misfortune, and tried to use that to make Delia see they could really have something together, be something together.

His grandmother used to tell him that the secret to a long and lasting relationship is *not* to remain in love with each other every day, because that just ain't the way it works. A lifetime is a *long* time. As you grow older, you change, and *all* of you grows and changes. This includes emotions. The secret, she had said, is to never give up on wooing the one you love. Woo them every day. Every single day. Because things can change.

So, all he'd been doing, really, was not giving up on Delia; he believed that sooner or later, he could get her emotions to change.

But his grandmother also told him that love is a blessing. Yes, it would mean heaven on earth if Delia reciprocates the feelings he has, but if she doesn't, well, he is still blessed to be able to experience love at all. To have his heart so full with such a graceful offering is something he will never dampen with wishful tears or heavy sighs.

He loves her, it's that simple.

And he wants to be able to thank her for that.

Because he is filled with blessed love. Even if she doesn't love him back right now, and even if that never changes.

'Any change?' Guy asks as he stares down at Delia.

And Shephard Rose answers, 'No,' even though Guy had not really been asking Shepherd at all.

chapter
twenty-seven

This is all my fault, Shepherd Rose thinks, as he watches his daughter breathe. 'They revived her easily enough,' he tells Guy, 'and that's a good sign. But, until she regains consciousness, and they can run some tests, they won't know how long she was without oxygen, and if she will be ...'

He can't say the words *brain damaged* out loud, because they just don't *fit* in a sentence about his beautiful, vibrant, amazing daughter.

'*If* she regains consciousness,' Imogen whispers from the corner of the room.

Shepherd has to bite his lip to keep control and refrain from slapping the woman clear across the room. Never before has he struck her, despite how much he may have wanted to, despite how much she had hurt him and how badly he had wanted to hurt her back. But every time he thought about what his wife had done to him, to them, every time he thought about leaving her, he would look over at the smiling face of Delia, and a part of him glowed with pure gratitude for the heartbreaking betrayal that had brought this ray of sunshine into his world. How could he hate Imogen for that, when he *loved* her so much for it? He would just never let his wife know it, and that would be her punishment. The guilt that ripped her open every day would be her punishment.

God, how could he have said such horrible things to Delia last night? *She's no daughter of mine! ... After I raised her and provided for her ...*

Of course Delia is *his* daughter, maybe not biologically, but he'd been there when she'd said her first word: *Dada.* He'd been there to teach her to crawl, to walk, to ride a bike. *He'd* been there to father her, not Morgan Starre. Delia is as much Shepherd's child, as is Claude.

And now, here they both are, in twin hospital beds, fighting for their lives. And the last words he'd said to each of them had been nasty.

Shepherd sees Claude's hurt and humiliated face at the wine launch, as he told him to get out of his sight; he sees the broken-hearted horror in Delia's eyes, as he had made her seem less important to him than money.

They say that to lose a child is the worst thing a parent can go through.

But that is simply not true.

Shepherd looks from one bed to the next and back again.

The worst thing a parent can go through, he thinks, is to lose them both.

chapter twenty-eight

This is all my fault.

Ben drives with his foot to the floor.

I should not have left her behind.

The outside world blurring and the harmonic shush of tyres in his ear doing nothing at all to calm him as he leaves behind this beautiful town, on which he hitched the plans of a clean slate, and a future with Delia. It was such stuff as dreams were made on. Dreams that were supposed to begin this very evening.

As he speeds through the day, he replays Puck's voicemail message again and again. Each word slices through his brain and he winces from the sharpness of them.

Delia is in the hospital. Sleeping pills. Coma. Possible brain damage. Sorry. Sorry, man. Sorry. This is all my fault.

So, yes, his dreams are supposed to begin tonight. And now, he may instead have nightmares. But either way, and in whatever form it takes, he will be with Delia tonight. He will be with her forever, just like they planned.

And just like in a dream, time becomes malleable. In a blink, he is at the hospital, shivering in the doorway of Delia's room. A dim lamp breeds oily shadows that slide and slink from bed to bed, like hungry souls, over the still bodies of the two people he has put here.

Claude lays pale and still in his bed, as if dead, while Delia is hooked up to a crowd of loud machines and tubes and wires. A monitor shows the bouncing ball of her heart, and throws a sickly green glow over the room, painting everything the colour of old rotting meat.

And sitting beside Delia, with his head resting on her chest, is the guy from the dance. Slowly, he lifts his head and fixes his eyes on Ben, frowning.

'What are *you* doing here? Haven't you done enough? Or have you come to finish what you started?' He stands. 'I'm calling security!'

'Wait, please!' Ben holds out a hand. 'I recognise you from the wine launch. You're Guy? You love her, too.'

Guy's hand halts as he reaches for the red emergency button. He frowns again. 'Love her, *too*? You mean, you know about ...' he steps forward and whispers, 'about *everything*?'

'Yeah,' Ben says, remembering the conversation he overheard while hiding in Delia's closet. 'I know about all that.'

Guy nods, sits, and looks back at Delia's face. 'Her

father thinks that is what pushed her over the edge. Which is fair enough. I mean, it must have been a pretty big shock.' He looks up at Ben then. 'This must be really hard for you. Finding out you have a sibling, only to possibly lose her before you can bond. I'm sorry. How long have you known Delia is your sister?'

'Sister?' The word feels hot on Ben's tongue, but he doesn't understand why.

And something is wrong with the floor, too; the whole thing starts giving way beneath him.

'Listen.' Guy's voice is soft. 'They say she's suffered brain damage and the chances of her waking are not good. With every passing minute,' his voice cracks, 'those chances decrease.'

The doorway swoops towards Ben, holding him upright.

'Her parents are devastated. Imogen has been sedated; Shepherd took her home to rest. They were going to call your father and let him know, too. Guess he has a right, since he is her biological father. Is that why you're here? Did your dad tell you to come?'

'Could I ...' Ben breathes the words, 'have some time alone with her?'

'Of course,' Guy says softly. 'You're her family, after all.'

As he passes, Guy rests a firm hand on Ben's shoulder and squeezes. 'I'll be in the lounge having a bad coffee. Take all the time you need. If you need a friend, just say the word, man, okay?' And when he leaves the room, he takes all the air along with him.

He gazes down at Delia and clearly sees the thin nose, high forehead, and dark brown eyes of his father.

chapter twenty-nine

Shepherd Rose sits rigid in his lounge room, staring at the blanched faces of the two people who have not been in this house since his daughter's conception.

'They're *married?*' whispers Morgan Starre.

'Are you sure?' asks Desdemona.

'Delia told Imogen last night,' Shepherd replies.

'And that's why Imogen told her about ...' Morgan looks down at his hands, 'about *me?*'

'Yes.'

'And that's why she ...?

'Your guess is as good as mine, Morgan, but it would make sense, wouldn't it?' Shepherd spits his words, using all his strength not to cross the room and punch Morgan Starre in the balls.

Desdemona shakes her head. 'I *knew* we should never have covered all this up! We should have just been honest right from the start, just like Morgan and I wanted. None of this would have happened.'

'What is that supposed to mean?' Shepherd asks her. 'That this is *my* fault?'

'Well, you're the one who begged us to keep the complete truth from Imogen all these years!' Desdemona stands. 'If she had known what *really* happened, do you think Delia would be in the hospital right now?'

'That's right.' Morgan stands as well, and shouts down at Shepherd. 'I mean, it's not like this is the first time Delia has attempted suicide, is it?'

'How dare you!' Shepherd launches from his seat, unable to contain the anger any longer, and as he balls his fists and steps towards Morgan, the phone rings, and they all freeze.

Shepherd answers it on the third ring, and as he listens, his jaws falls open.

Holding up a hand to silence Morgan's questions, he presses the receiver closer to his ear to make sure he's heard the words spoken on the other end correctly. 'Thank you for letting me know,' he says finally, and lets the phone drop.

'Is it Delia?' asks Morgan.

'Is she ...?' Desdemona's face pales.

Shepherd shakes his head at them. 'Delia is fine,' he says. 'It's uh ...' He clears his throat. 'It's *Ben*, actually.'

'What about him?' asks Desdemona, clutching at her husband's hand.

'That was Guy Shylock on the phone. Ben has come back. He is at the hospital right now, he's in with Delia.'

'And so he *should* be!' says Morgan. 'She *is* his wife after all.'

For a long moment, Shepherd stares at Morgan, not really sure how to say the next words. 'He *knows*, Morgan.' Shepherd's voice is thin and weak. 'Guy thought he already knew, and he mentioned something. Ben knows that you are Delia's biological father.'

'So, he must think that she's his ... *sister?*' Morgan sits down.

'Oh no,' whispers Desdemona. 'Call the hospital. Get him on the phone right now.'

'No,' says Morgan and he looks at Shepherd. 'This is not the kind of conversation to have over the phone. He deserves to hear the truth in person. From you, Shepherd. Ben deserves to hear the truth, finally, from his *real* father.'

chapter thirty

Shepherd Rose stared at his wife, who sat across the breakfast table with tears dripping onto her untouched plate of food.

'But this is wonderful news,' he said, rising from his chair. 'Why do you seem so sad? We've always planned on having more children. A little brother or sister for Claudey.'

Imogen's face crumpled further. She dropped her face into her hands, as if unable to hold her head up any longer.

In that second, something clicked into place for Shepherd. He stopped halfway around the table and rested his hands upon its steady surface. Frowning, he thought back over the past few months, trying to remember the last time his wife had kissed him, let alone done anything that would result in a pregnancy.

He counted back the weeks, the months.

And then he said, 'Oh.' And then he sat on the

nearest chair. And then he placed his face in his hands, too, so he didn't have to look at his wife any longer. 'Whose is it?'

The whisper of the name was tiny, but the weight of it crushed him nevertheless.

He looked up. 'My best friend?'

'I'm so sorry, Shepherd, it just ...'

'It just what? Don't you dare say it just *happened*, Imogen. Jesus Christ! You don't just have sex with your husband's best friend – with your best friend's husband – by accident!'

'I'm sorry,' she said again. 'I don't know what else I can say.'

'Good,' he said. 'Because I don't know if I want to listen to you anymore.' He headed for the foyer, snatched up his keys, and let the echo of the slamming door slap Imogen in the face.

As he sped to Morgan's house, he didn't know what he wanted to say. If he wanted to say anything at all. If he wanted to just punch the man who had slept with his wife.

How could this have happened? How could the two people he loved most have betrayed him so fiercely? Morgan had been like a brother to him for so many years. And Imogen – his beautiful, beloved Imogen – had been the best thing that had ever happened to him. Their love had been instant, and strong, and unwavering all this time. Perfect. At least, he'd thought it had been perfect.

True, he had been spending more time in the office these past few months. Whenever he had come home early enough to spend time with her, he'd ended up falling asleep. But she understood. She said she understood all that. She knew he was doing all this for her! Working so hard for her! For them! For their future! He was doing all this because he loved her so very much, to give her the kind of life she deserved, to prove to her that she was the most important thing in his world.

And how did she repay him?

Shepherd felt the sting of tears and pulled the car over. He hunched into himself as the sobs shook his body and the pain of this betrayal sliced up his heart.

He was crying so loudly that at first he didn't hear the tapping of fingernails on his window, but when he heard someone callling his name, he wiped his hands over his wet cheeks and looked up.

'Jesus,' he muttered, as he opened the door and stepped out. Then, he tried to smile and said, 'Hi, Desdemona,' but the words came out all choked up.

'Oh, Shepherd, are you all right?'

He shook his head, no, and bit his bottom lip.

'What on earth is the matter?'

At this question, he laughed. A short, shocked laugh, at first. And then a long, drawn out guffaw, that rolled into a belly laugh, until eventually, Desdemona was laughing right along with him.

At the sight of Desdemona Starre, hunched over, with

tears of laughter splashing onto her running shoes, Shepherd stopped laughing and straightened up because this was not funny, this was not funny at all, and she deserved to know the truth, and, well, Shepherd wanted to get a little bit of revenge against his so-called best friend.

'Imogen slept with Morgan,' he said. 'And she's pregnant with his child.'

Desdemona stopped and looked at him for a beat, frowned slightly, and then she started laughing again, harder than before.

But when he did not join her, Desdemona's laughter faded for good.

She stared at him for a very long time, searching his eyes. And then she nodded. One quick, simple nod, before stepping forward to kiss him.

chapter thirty-one

Hot tears spill along the hill of Ben's nose and drop onto Delia's pillow with the soft sound of realisation.

'I understand,' he whispers. 'I know why you did it. Your heart, like mine, was made to love. And if it can't love completely, then it can't beat at all. I think you might be right, my love.'

She tried to kill herself. And he totally gets it. If she cannot live without him, if she is brave enough to make that kind of sacrifice, then what right does he have to continue living without her?

Death may be our only answer. In death, he will not be Ben, and she will not be Delia. No teeth, no eyes, no taste, no everything. In death, they will be without bodies; without a shared blood that runs in the veins of their shared father. In death, they will be nothing but two souls who are destined to be together.

'The course of true love never did run smooth,' he

whispers, brushing his fingers through her hair, 'but at least in death we will finally be together.'

Maybe love does conquer all. Even death.

In the empty corridor, Ben listens for the soft approach of rubber-soled shoes. He tries the door to the janitor's closet and is surprised to find it unlocked. The strong scent of chemicals reaches up and scratches his nostrils and eyes and mouth with sharp fingernails.

From a high shelf, Ben takes down a bottle of bleach and turns it over to read: *Poison. Harmful if swallowed. Do not induce vomiting. Seek medical attention immediately. Do not mix with other household chemicals such as ammonia.*

He reaches for a bottle of ammonia, and joy spreads warm in his chest, as if this cocktail is already coursing through him.

But when he turns to leave, he is blocked in by a huge figure in the doorway.

'What you doing in here?' The janitor steps forward and snatches the bottles from Ben's weak grasp.

'I ... I was just uh ...'

'You was just nicking stuff, weren't you?' says the janitor. 'I leave the door unlocked for two minutes whiles I go to have a piss, and this is what happens! You realise, if stuff goes missing on my shift, that I have to pay for it? You think I can afford to do that? My little girl's birthday next week, you know, and I'm trying to save up to buy her a bicycle! Been putting money aside every week for it; been going without me cigarettes, I have, just so I could save up the money! A bike's all she been asking for, it is. And now you shows up to nick my supplies, so I'll have to pay for them out of her bike money, which means I won't be able to make the last payment in time for her birthday.'

'I'm sorry, sir,' Ben says.

'I should tell security on you, I should.'

If this guy calls security, Ben will be marched straight to Burgundy's office. 'I can pay you.'

'Pay me?' says the janitor. 'Why can't you just go and buy your own cleaning stuff, instead of buying mine?'

Ben fumbles for his wallet and slides out all the cash he has – he won't need it anymore – and presses it against the janitor's wide chest.

'Four hundred?' gasps the janitor, counting the notes. 'Just for a bottle of bleach and window cleaner?' He leans down and whispers, 'Should you be walking around in here? You haven't escaped from the loony ward downstairs, have you?'

But if the janitor thinks Ben is a crazy person, he doesn't let that cloud his judgement. He frees his hands of the bottles in order to close his fingers around the cash. Yet he still does not move from the doorway.

'What you want them for so bad anyway?' he asks. 'You aren't going to do anything, you know, *stupid*, to yourself, are you?'

'This money will get your daughter her bike, plus a helmet, knee pads, and a pretty basket with a big plastic flower on it.' Ben smiles. 'Don't worry about me.'

The janitor folds the notes, steps aside, and looks away as Ben heads back down the hall to Delia and Claude's room.

Wedging a chair against the door, he takes a moment to stare at Delia; her chest rising and falling with the mechanical rapidity of the machine that breathes for her, the line of green light jumping in perfect rhythm to her heart that has lost all happy desire to beat. This room is no longer a breeder of life, but a womb of death, pregnant with the most beautiful embryo of all, and soon to be the proud carrier of twins.

Or even, he blinks over at Claude, triplets.

'Well, old rival, this is my gift to you: your killer is about to be avenged.'

Approaching Delia's side again, Ben places the two bottles on the shelf beside her. He touches a hand to her soft cheek, so beautiful even in the face of death.

Is it possible that she could still wake and be perfectly herself again? Guy had said the chances weren't good, but a chance was a chance, was it not? But then, what if she did regain consciousness, and had to live the rest of her life in some special care facility for the brain-damaged? She wouldn't want to live a life trapped inside a body that was no longer working; it would be hell enough to live without a heart that was no longer able to love.

In the corner of the room is a small sink, and Ben takes the bouquet of white roses over to it, and empties the water down the drain. He then unscrews the lids of the bleach and ammonia, and pours both into the empty vase. The acrid smell fills the room and he is not sure if his tears flow now from grief or from the fumes.

'Delia,' he whispers, 'I don't know if you can hear me, but we'll be together very soon.'

**

Surrounded by a smoke-like darkness that curls around her and into her very being, Delia floats in the void between asleep and awake. It is warm and comforting here. No pain, no heartache, no tears. She sinks deeper into the blackness, becomes wrapped tighter in its folds, until a voice penetrates through the depths and she slowly rises to the surface, buoyed by its familiar timbre.

**

Through his burning tears, Ben tries to focus on Delia's face. He reaches his arm across her chest for one last embrace. Then, with his hands placed gently on her cheeks, Ben turns her face to his. He slides the thin oxygen tube out of Delia's slender throat and a high-pitched beep squeals through the room.

Delia's lips, those two crimson doors through which breath has come and gone so easily, Ben now seals closed with one last kiss, as her body begins to buck beneath him, fighting to stay alive.

'Here's to you, my love.' And then in one long swallow that ignites his throat, Ben seals his fate.

**

Delia has heard other voices in this comfortable place, but those voices had been muffled, filtered. They had no power or ability to penetrate this world of all-encompassing blackness. But *his* voice, coupled with love's translations, pierced the dark like a flaming arrow, straight and true.

He is here.

And she needs to get back to him. Now. Whatever the consequences may be, she doesn't want to leave him behind.

Layer by layer, Delia peels away the darkness, and she crawls back up towards the light, back up towards life, and back up towards Ben.

**

Ben's mouth blisters instantly, and his throat closes with the force of a slamming door. He gasps like a drowning fish as he clutches himself to Delia, and together they both stop breathing.

**

She is being held under water. She is being pounded against the sandy bottom of the ocean floor. She is staring helplessly up at the swirling, foaming surface above. Every time she kicks her way up and is just inches away from breaking the surface and drinking in a mouthful of clean sweet oxygen, another wave crashes down on her and she somersaults back to the bottom, gulping in only cold, salty brine.

A high-pitched whine screeches above the waves like seagulls.

A loud banging, over and over, shattering glass, the sound of a door crashing against a wall.

More voices now. Urgent voices. And her father shouting for help.

'What's that smell?'

'Someone open a window!'

'Get him off her!'

'Her oxygen tube has been removed!'

'Look, she's breathing on her own!'

Cold fingertips force Delia's eyelids apart and she blinks into a flashlight beam.

'She's responsive!'

'Can you tell me your full name, honey?'

Delia tries to speak, but she can't get the words to form.

'Don't move,' someone says. 'Just lay still, relax.'

'Who *is* this guy?'

'He's not breathing.'

'Looks like he's been into the supplies cupboard; drank a cocktail of bleach and ammonia.'

'We need to get him into ER now! Get a gurney in here!'

The urgency of these voices, and more so, the *lack* of Ben's, slaps Delia hard. She forces her eyes to focus and fights the arms that try to keep her still. 'Ben?' she croaks, and speaking his name out loud gives her a jolt of energy. 'Ben?'

She turns her face towards a whoosh of air as a gurney is whisked past her into the hall, and in that flash of movement, she sees his white face and blue lips beneath an oxygen mask. A doctor straddles Ben's chest, pumping his hands rhythmically against it.

Beside her, a stunned nurse holds two empty bottles of cleaning fluid.

Oh, Ben, thinks Delia, what did you do? Poison yourself? You summon me back to full consciousness by the sheer sound of your voice, only to leave me here with no way to follow you.

Laying her head back on the starched pillow, Delia weeps. Her eyes overflow with hot salty brine, drowning herself, returning her to that warm world of watery nothingness where Ben will now be waiting for her.

epilogue

Ben watches it all unfold, horrified, and unable to stop her.

Poison had taken him away from her. Poison, all of which he had selfishly drunk, leaving not a drop to allow her to follow him. And now, she has to find a new means.

Her shaking fingers grip the handle of a gleaming knife so tight her knuckles whiten. In the hallway outside, voices approach, and Ben wishes he could call out to them, to scream at them to hurry up, hurry up and stop her!

And in that moment, she hears them too. She pauses for just a second and stares at the doorway, before looking back down at the dagger in her fist.

'Then I'll be brief,' she says to the knife, as if it were not just a piece of sharpened metal designed to dissect, but a friendly guide that will reunite her with love. 'Oh, happy dagger, this is thy sheath.'

Ben cries out as she embeds the blade into her stomach so deep that only the handle is visible.

She gasps in pain and Ben echoes her, a guttural, horrified rasp, although of course she doesn't hear him.

Her body starts to shiver.

As she curls herself around the pooling blood, she whispers to the knife one more time. 'Rust there and let me die.'

Beside Ben, Delia sniffs and wipes her face against his shirt.

'Hey!' he hisses, 'I'm not your tissue, you know.'

'No, but you are my husband, and that means I can use you for any purpose I see fit.'

Ben hands her a tissue and drops a kiss on her brow before turning back to face the stage, upon which Juliet – played by Katherine – is dying so heart-breakingly well.

'She's very good isn't she,' he says.

'Of course,' says Delia. 'She's the best.'

This special showing of *Romeo and Juliet* is being performed on the back lawn of the new Starre-Rose estate, as part of the launch of their first wine, Pink Peace.

On either side of Ben and Delia sit their families, and on either side of their families sit almost the entire town. Everyone has come together to celebrate, not only the wine, but the peace and love that now joins the Starres and the Roses.

And right at the back of this crowd, in the shadow of a

large tree, I sit unnoticed, gazing around me at the people of this town.

A month has passed since I sat in my velvet tent and predicted this entire occurrence. A whole month since I made up a prophecy and watched it unfold around me, like the scenes in a play.

The skin around Ben's mouth is pink and puckered with scar tissue, and his voice has a gravelly rasp that will never smooth over. Now, because of me, with every word Ben Starre speaks, he will appreciate the fragility of life and the wonder of love, both of which he came so close to losing.

Delia recovered completely from her coma; she had been deemed fit to return home only three days after waking, with no temporary or permanent damage. She too, because of me, is now keenly aware of the importance of living life to the fullest.

Although Claude is still undergoing rehabilitation therapy for a shattered kneecap, he has recovered from his accident – both physically and emotionally. Today, he sits with his head bowed in brotherly laughter with Orlando Starre, whose fingers are entwined with those of Ross Aylind in open and public affection.

I am warm and glowing as I survey all the lives that I have changed, while on stage, staring down at the dead bodies of Romeo and Juliet, Escalus, the Prince of Verona, turns to face the crowd. His arms reach out, imploring. 'A glooming peace this morning with it brings.

The sun, for sorrow, will not show his head. Go hence to have more talk of these sad things. Some shall be pardoned and some punished. For never was a story of more woe than that of Juliet and her Romeo.'

The entire town rises as one to applaud the end of this famous and tragic play, unaware of how close they came to a similar end. In the front row, Guy Shylock lays a bouquet of roses at Katherine's feet. She bends to pick them up, blushes, and blows him a kiss as the crowd claps louder.

The people of this town, who are now freed from the poisonous hatred of two feuding families, celebrate and shake hands and clink glasses in brotherhood, and still no one notices me as I stand and turn and leave this place.

In my left hand, my crystal ball catches the sunlight, which swirls and plinks inside the glass like a moth against a window, or perhaps like destiny, eager to break free and influence the future of the next soul to whom I will attach it.